CARL GOES TO MOUSE WORLD

by

RJ Richards

To: Adler Leo,

Happy 5ᵗʰ Birthday.

May all of your wishes come true!

Your friend,

RJ Richards

Dedicated to everyone who believed in me. You know who you are.-RJR

1
Living the Life

That mouse thinks he is so clever. I was keeping an eye on the hole in the wall because I knew sooner or later he would stick his little head out to get the lay of the land. He smelled the air a few times in an attempt to figure out just where I might be, but it won't matter. I'm on top of my human's couch and neatly disguised since my beautiful brown coat matches the color of the couch itself. I keep perfectly still as he starts to inch away from his hole. He's nervous, as he remembers how close I came to snatching him during our last encounter. He stops and smells the air again, tempted by the cracker crumbs one of humans dropped on the floor. He darts to the first crumb where he quickly devours it. Oh, this will be too easy. *Keep eating my fat little mouse, it will just make you that much slower.*

I slink down to the arm rest and watch as he moves towards a large crumb resting on the floor. He is farther from his little home than he has been in sometime, but he can't pass up this unexpected treat. The humans usually disgust me with their messes, but at least this is one mess that will serve me well. I drop to the floor as a loud vehicle passes by to mask any noise I might make. It works, as my hungry prey moves to yet another crunchy crumb. Oh, it's hard not think about the little snack I will soon be having. Should I have mouse on a stick? Perhaps, a mouse burger? I could simply showcase him to my human and be rewarded with a nice chicken dish from the can. Oh, how I love wet food. Humans say the canned food stinks, but I think of them as simply heavenly. I inch closer and closer and the mouse still doesn't hear me. My hunting skills are perfect as usual. I am a simple swat away from ending this, when the mouse freezes and smells the air. My superior hearing picks up his heart as it races. He knows I'm close. I unleash my claws and rear back my paw when...

"Carl! Wake up, you sleepy cat!" The human male yells out as he moves in and picks me up. Another perfect dream ruined. I go limp and let him have his few minutes of love. He gives me the usual routine and I just yawn and take it all in.

"You lazy cat, you've been sleeping all day."

"You're getting fat. You fat cat. Are you a fat cat?"

"Kitty going to get a mouse today? Kitty better catch me a mouse today."

"Meow, meow. Come on, Carl, meow, meow."

I do what all cats do and go through the motions. I rub up against his leg and do a little purring. It's not that I don't care for the humans in my home, but the routine gets old. I want a little adventure in my life, as being a house cat can get boring. I look out the window and see the street cats having all the fun. They sing to the lady cats at all hours of the night, they tease the chained-up dogs, and they get to tear up all the flower beds in the neighborhood. Me? I sleep twenty-three hours a day, take a few baths, and eat my usual bowl of dry tuna-flavored food. I'm not exactly Mr. Exciting.

Oh sure, I have some fun. My human family usually likes to have dinner around six o'clock and I make sure to time my litter box visit right about then just to mess with them. The human male likes to cuddle up next to the human female when the kids go to sleep and I always jump between them or walk on them to make sure they know who truly rules this den. The kids are the best. They're usually willing to hold me, even though they just put on their church clothes. It's great, I leave my old hair on their clothes and they get yelled at by the adult human female. Yes, I have my fun, but I'm ready for some new challenges. Oh, and the mouse dream I had earlier? Just a dream, this house doesn't even have a bug in it, let alone a mouse. How's a master hunter supposed to do his thing if there's nothing to hunt? It's pathetic.

You see, it never used to be like this for us. Cats have been honored for centuries, but it seems like the respect given to us lessens more all the time. My mother, the Queen, used to tell me about the Egyptian cats who were honored as royalty. The Egyptian humans of that time must have been extremely intelligent. Cats were recognized as being superior to all other creatures on Earth. They probably praised them for their unique beauty and marveled at their extreme power. Clearly, they knew that we were equals to our cousins the lion and tiger. They were some of the few humans who seemed to "get it." I think of those times and just have to sigh. It must have been so exhilarating to live back in that day.

My Queen had confidence I would live a good life, but there were no guarantees. She said every one of her kittens would be adopted, but it would be the luck of the draw as to where each one would go. Some would go off in a cardboard box to one of the local stores where they would shop for their humans. Some would get lucky and go to a home with lots of food and toys where they would be constantly praised. They might have to put up with an older human female who put clothes on them or kept squeezing them, but at least their bellies were full. Some would get a nice farm where they could hunt mice, snakes, and bugs and be recognized by the humans as the protector of the land. They had large territories to patrol but always had to beware of dogs and rivals that always seemed to be lurking. Some led horrible lives where they were ignored and given only token scraps. I would hear horror stories where they were filthy and sick, reduced to skin and bones. Most of us fell into the category I called my own, where I selected a human family that basically treated me nicely and for the most part took care of my needs, but… they were extremely boring. Humans usually are boring, in case you didn't know. Thus, my life became extremely boring.

The Queen told me it was a game of chance where humans were concerned. Sometimes you just have to accept the fact that not all of us will strike it rich. I'm just grateful that our Egyptian ancestors can't see us now. They would be disgusted. They would wonder how we could wreck something so perfect.

I shouldn't complain too much. My humans aren't that bad. They showered me with attention when I was a kitten. They knew I was upset to have to leave the Queen and they gave me lots of love and snacks. They complimented me on my brown patterns and my little pink stomach. The kids would always fight with each other so they could hold and kiss me. I was truly beginning to think that I won the jackpot, but then reality set in. I began to grow up and suddenly, I went from cute to fat. Without warning, my late night noises went from funny to aggravating. I went from having a healthy appetite to being compared to a pig. A pig? Can you imagine? Since when is someone who for all intents and purposes is a lion, suddenly a pig? It's insulting to be sure. But what could I do? They were my humans and I was stuck with them. Yes, I could eat them if I desired, but I'm just too nice for my own good.

After much self-reflection, I've decided I need a vacation. I need a little excitement in my life. Maybe I could find a nice tuna factory to visit or perhaps a good old chicken farm would be the ticket.

Oh, who am I kidding? I'm a realist. I'm stuck here and I might as well get used to it. A vacation? Some adventure? Nah, it will never happen.

2

An Unpleasant Discovery

Dogs always get the credit for being master detectives and courageous explorers, but the reality is that the cat is far greater at both. No, we don't lend ourselves out to the humans to sniff out unpleasant things and we don't glamorize our adventures to the Hollywood crowd. We use our unique talents to better the Cat World, because, let's be serious; the Cat World is the one that matters most.

Sometimes when the family is away, I like to investigate and explore our home. It is in times like these that I might discover where the human male is hiding a snack or where the kids have stashed away a toy. I like to find these things and see the shock on the human's faces when they can't find their little treasures.

The human male is my favorite. He will reach his hand to the side of his chair where he hides his precious bag of jerky and then have a comically puzzled look on his face when he sees it is nearly empty. I'm sure he thinks the human female or the kids found his prize and devoured it, but he doesn't want to accuse anyone, so he lets it go.

The kids are especially funny as they go to pull out their new prized toy to show a friend only to discover that it has a hole in it. I like to bite their new toys, as it feels good on my teeth, and there is the added amusement of seeing their friends trying to figure out why they are being presented something that is obviously broken. The children usually blame each other and many of these disagreements can be quite amusing to me.

Does anyone ever blame the cat? No, of course not. They just think I'm a fat and lazy kitty cat who wouldn't be bothered with such things as tasty jerky or a prized new toy. Despite the satisfaction this gives me, even these incidents have grown boring to me. It's just too easy.

One particular morning, after the family had departed for church, I decided to go on a patrol of my territory. I thought I might explore the kitchen cupboards or maybe even see if I could figure out why that water drips out of the faucet in the human litter room. Perhaps I would go chew on some of the human female's plants just to mess with her head a little. It was during my expedition that I came across something most unsettling. On the kitchen cupboard was a booklet with a large grey mouse on the cover. This booklet was advertising some kind of vacation paradise called Mouse World and was apparently run by this large mouse that was named Marvin Mouse. Marvin Mouse? This is ridiculous. Since when do mice run human vacation resorts? Since when do mice get so big? Something is definitely wrong in the world.

I decided to put the vacation booklet into perspective. *After all, it doesn't really mean anything. The humans get all kinds of paper literature in the mail and either throw it away or line my litter box with it. I'm not going to let this particular brochure bother me.* At least, this is what I was still telling myself when I overheard the kids talking about Marvin Mouse in their bedroom later that evening.

"Can you believe we get to see Marvin Mouse?" Hailey said to her sister Sydney in an excited voice.

"I want to see his wife Mary Mouse, too." Sydney was giggling and seemed to be on the verge of hysteria. *Did she say Mary Mouse? Since when do mice have wives?* Suddenly I had a big headache.

I spent most of the evening in heavy thought, sitting under the kitchen table (or what I call one of my "dens"). I honestly couldn't remember my Queen ever mentioning any kind of giant mouse. I mean, if there was such a giant mouse, every cat in the world would be trying to catch it. The thought of dragging that oversized mouse to my humans and them lavishing me with praise for being the world's greatest hunter excited me to no end.

The next morning, I heard Sydney ask the human male when they would be going to see Marvin Mouse. The human, as always, had a mouth full of food, but I believe he said next week. Next week? For a cat, that would feel like a few years, but it was still too close for comfort. My humans were actually going to see this mouse and they were excited about it. This mouse would receive the praise and love that I deserved. It was I who brought some class and royalty to this household. It was I who was clearly the most beautiful thing in their lives. It was I who would have gladly hunted any mouse, snake, or bug that entered into this home. It was so typical of the humans to forget that I so generously let them pet me and I am always so kind to help eat their food. I should go up to the human male and swat him, but I am too distressed. Are they really going to pick this Marvin Mouse over me? I'll be the laughing stock of cats everywhere.

This situation has gone on long enough. It is eating my insides. I barely ate two bowls of food because I am so stressed out. I only managed to sleep twenty one hours and could barely get through six baths. I needed answers. I needed my friends. I think it's about time that I had a little party.

3

The Cat Summit

Cats have a very unique leadership structure. You see there are some humans who stick to the whole, King-of-the-Jungle thing when describing our large cousin, the Lion. They think that the Lion is the king of all cats and that they deserve all the respect in the world. Others just separate the "domestic cat" from the "big cats". Big cats are the leopards, lions, tigers, and other forest and jungle dwelling feline predators. Still other humans, the smarter ones, I might add, understand that the domestic cat is the smartest and most beautiful of all cats and therefore, *they* are the kings of cats. More than likely, humans, with this wisdom, are descendants of the Egyptians.

Now, domestic cats don't have a chain of command, per se, instead, they independently run their own households or territories. The household that has more than one cat will see the older and stronger alpha male hold the leadership role in most cases. In a neighborhood of outside cats, you might see numerous border skirmishes and hear heated battles in the night, but generally, each cat respects the territorial integrity of the other. For the most part, we're all quite friendly with one another. Even I, a house cat, have managed to gain several fine friends through windowsill conversations.

My best friend is named Rex. I know, I know, it is a traditional dog name, but, due to some sick humor from his human, he had it bestowed upon him. Rex has one of those humans that would name his cat "Rex", his dog "Morris", and his goldfish "Fido". Humans, truly do have, a twisted sense of humor. Regardless, Rex is a six-year-old apple head Siamese. He is an outside cat for the most part and is a great hunter.

Well, to be honest, I have never even seen any evidence of one of his kills, but he tells great hunting stories. For an inside cat, hunting stories can be quite the treat and I always enjoy hearing them from Rex.

Cindy is a four-year-old grey Western Siberian with a beautiful thick coat and an appetite for any kind of bread or cheese. I would sometimes let her hop through the window and patrol under the kitchen table the day after the kids enjoyed a toasted cheese sandwich. More often than not, Cindy came away licking her lips from a morsel that made it to the floor. Cindy is a lazy cat, but she is usually kind enough to fill me in on her adventures near the creek where she can usually be found hunting frogs and lizards.

There is also a young brown tabby named Mars. Mars has a human who loves chocolate bars and named his new cat after one of his favorites. Somehow the name fits Mars, as he was slightly "out-to-space", so to speak. One time, I heard a fire truck racing down the road only to find out later that it was sent to retrieve Mars from a tree after he had gotten stuck in it. There was another time when

Mars came to visit and his hair was all out of sorts. He told me that he fell in the human litter bowl and soaked himself. Disgusting, but I have to admit it was a little funny.

The day of the summit, I felt like I needed my friends. Since the humans were heading off to work and school, I decided to extend the invite. As soon as I heard the human car pull out of the driveway, I raced to the window and began calling. I sang out beautiful meows and before too long, I was answered by return calls and the neighborhood dog population barking up a storm. These dogs don't have any taste at all.

As a good host, I brought out some of my better squeaking toys and even saved a little bit of my chicken and rice formula for anyone who might want a nibble. Knowing my friends, this snack wouldn't last long. I wanted the mood to be just right because I didn't know exactly how they would react when I brought up the subject of a giant mouse that the humans apparently loved.

Rex was the first to show up and, as usual, he was in a frisky mood. I said "hello" to him and he replied with a head butt and clawless swat to my side.

"Rex, I don't have time to wrestle with you right now. This meeting is serious."

Rex moved his head to the side and looked somewhat confused, "Serious? What happened, did your humans decide to make your tail into a stub?"

"That's not funny, Rex. You'll have to wait until the rest of our group gets here and then I'll fill you in."

Rex decided to await the rest of the group with a quick claw sharpening on my humans couch. Normally I would rebuke him, since I will be the one to get blamed, but I had to stay focused. A fight with my best friend would disrupt the whole meeting.

Cindy was the next to show up, and without even a friendly greeting, she began to sniff the air.

"I left some of my breakfast in the bowl if you are interested," I offered.

"It smells like regular cat food. I was hoping for some cheese or maybe even a little bit of bagel," she replied as she began her walk to my bowl and started to devour the food.

"Well, it didn't take you long to settle, did it?"

Cindy smiled as she crunched and replied, "A girl has to keep her energy levels up."

I figured Mars would be the last to arrive and sure enough he was late. He jumped into the house and tracked mud everywhere.

"Mars! What are you doing? You are leaving muddy paw prints everywhere!" I yelled, but Mars looked at me like I was the crazy one.

"What's the big deal, Carl? It's only mud. I was down at the creek cooling off my paws."

Cindy jumped in, "Cooling off your paws? Mars, you're a cat, not a simple dog who takes a dip in a dirty creek."

Mars was Mars and just smiled as he took a seat awaiting the meeting. Realizing Mars would never give an intelligent reply, Cindy took a seat beside him.

"Rex, are you coming or are you going to keep scratching up my couch?" I asked my friend as he continued to tear the couch to shreds.

"To be honest, I have the urge to keep tearing up the couch. But since you said this is important, I'll sit down," he replied in his matter of fact way.

I had a little bit of stage fright as I looked into the eyes of my three friends. Rex had the probing and curious eyes of a cat in his prime, Cindy had the eyes of cat who was disinterested in everything but food and praise, and Mars…well, Mars had a vacant look on his face.

"My friends, I have brought you all together today to discuss something so disturbing that it will likely rattle your very core," I said to set the stage.

"Don't tell me there is a ban on cheese!" Cindy said with her eyes wide open.

"I'm worried they will require all cats to be on leashes," Mars said with a look of fear on his face.

"Cats, cats, let Carl talk. You're both acting crazy. As long as he's not going to tell us that mice have gone extinct, I'm not worried," Rex said with confidence.

"Well, it's not the mice I'm worried about going extinct, old buddy…it's the…it's the…" I couldn't seem to bring myself to say it.

"It's the dogs who are going extinct, isn't it?" Rex asked. "Ha ha, I knew they didn't have it in them for the long haul."

All of a sudden, Cindy seemed to be taking interest when the look of fear seemed to take her over. "No, Rex, I don't think he's talking about the dogs. Are you talking about what I think you're talking about?"

I swallowed and said, "Yes, I'm talking about the end of us. I'm talking about the end of all cats."

4

Marvin Mouse

Now, any time you tell a cat that their very existence is in jeopardy, a certain kind of panic can ensue. The rumor that we have nine lives is untrue, so any threat to our continued presence makes us sweat.

"OK, calm down, calm down," I pleaded as they circled with their tales wagging like crazy. The tail is important to watch and has resulted in a lot of people being bitten. Unlike the dog, we don't wag our tail when we're happy.

Cindy was the first to snap at me, "Calm down? Calm down? What kind of danger are we in?"

Rex followed, "Yeah, buddy, this is crazy. What's going on?"

I swallowed hard. "It involves a giant mouse that the humans apparently love." This stopped the three in their tracks. After looking at one another, they all fell onto their backs laughing up a storm. I felt as though my friends were either out of their minds or I was a victim of a very cruel joke.

Rex was the first to speak up, "Are you talking about Marvin Mouse? Carl, he's been around for years. He's not even real."

Cindy weighed in next, "Carl, there is no such thing as a giant mouse! You've been hitting the cat nip again, haven't you?"

I couldn't take it anymore. "Now, wait a second. I know a mouse when I see one!"

"No offense, buddy, but you don't ever get to go hunting. The only mice you see are in your dreams. You're an inside cat," Rex said with words that stung to my core.

Mars was silent for awhile but finally spoke up. "I wasn't the sharpest cat in my litter, but it could be possible for a giant mouse to exist. I mean, most of the dogs I see are little poodles and terriers, but there are times I see gigantic dogs pulling their humans."

"Hmmm...well, I can't discount that," Cindy said with her head cocked to the side.

"The humans had a brochure and there was a picture of a giant grey mouse that apparently runs some kind of resort for humans. The humans seem to love this place," I told my now attentive audience.

"They're probably brainwashing the humans. They aren't very smart, you know," Rex said nodding his head.

"I haven't told you the rest. I overheard the human children talking about a Mary Mouse," I told them, trying to drive home the point that there were two of these giant monstrosities.

Cindy looked scared as she said, "Oh dear, this could mean a whole family of giant mice! I'm talking about giant mice that are changing the way our humans think!"

Mars started tensing up and seemed to be paralyzed with fear, "I...I...I..."

Rex jumped over to him and gave him a head butt. "Don't you worry, Mars, I'll think of something."

I couldn't imagine what we could do, but Rex at least provided some comfort to our group. Maybe there was something we could do. I mean, after all, we are cats. We are superior to humans, dogs, and, of course, mice.

Cindy walked to the window and started to call. She sang out with beautiful meows of different tones in an effort to reach a yet unknown entry into our group. Soon, a faint meow came and I saw a large chubby calico leap into my home. It was Lilly Mae, one of the wisest cats around. She had spent two months imprisoned at something called an animal shelter and had developed a quick temper. She had vowed that upon release she would never miss another meal, so she had bulked up to twenty pounds of intimidating chubbiness. Well, at least I was intimidated.

"Guys, you all know my good friend Ms. Lilly Mae," said Cindy.

"Hmm…so this is the group of friends you always tell me about," Lilly Mae said as she scanned the room.

"We are in need of some advice, Lilly Mae. I thought that you might be the only cat wise enough to help us," Cindy said, playing to Lilly Mae's ego.

"Well, you thought right, Cindy. I know about as much as any cat can possibly know. I've been chased by every kind of dog imaginable and, at times, I even chased them back. I've been accused of being a bobcat or a mountain lion and, in one case, even a pig. I find that quite insulting by the way. I am a true cat genius," Lilly Mae said with her nose high in the air.

"Well, I'm sure you are, Lilly, and we are in desperate need of your expertise. You see, we're trying to learn more about a certain Marvin Mouse," I told our rotund guest.

Lilly Mae's eyes widened and the hair on the back of her neck stood up. She arched her back and let out a frightening hiss. Poor Mars fell off his chair backwards to the floor below.

"Did you say Marvin Mouse?" Lilly asked in a fiery tone. She began to pace and her claws came unsheathed. She started to scratch the human dinner table, but I felt that taking the blame from the humans was better than challenging this large cat.

"That's what we said, now what do you know about him?" Rex asked bravely.

Lilly Mae seemed to regain her composure and told us the story of Marvin Mouse. "From what I know, Marvin and his wife Mary run a human vacation resort. They are two of the wealthiest mice on Earth and, due to this wealth; they have grown to giant size. They eat the finest cheese in the world and it has helped them to grow beyond what we would call a big mouse. Their wealth and fame has thrust them into the human world and even helped them to learn the human language. Children everywhere love them and even bring home clothing bearing their likeness, movies that chronicle their adventures, and masks with their ugly faces on them! But I can tell you this, for every human child who loves these mice, there is a cat dreaming of the day when they can catch them!"

"But Lilly Mae, how can any cat hope to catch such large mice?" I asked with a touch of depression in my voice.

Lilly Mae looked me over and shook her head, "It wouldn't be easy for even me and it is likely impossible for a house cat like yourself. When was the last time you pursued a pigeon or tried to pounce on a rat?"

All eyes were on me as I searched my mind for an answer. "I....well...you see...I once...", I simply did not have an answer. Despite all of my dreams and fantasies, I simply didn't have much hunting experience. If I had never caught a young and dumb mouse, how could I catch a giant intelligent mouse?

Thankfully, Rex made the save. "Lilly Mae, it doesn't matter what Carl has or hasn't hunted. What matters is that you tell us how we should go about dealing with a giant mouse that has the love and attention of the humans. I mean, if Carl's humans turn their love to a mouse, my humans could as well."

"Or me," Cindy added.

"Even me...I mean, my human child is three now. Pretty soon he could be wearing mouse ears and forgetting all about me," Mars added.

Mars was right. The humans could push me out and continue their silly pursuit of this mouse. We needed action and we needed it soon.

"Lilly Mae, tell us how to get these giant mice!" I blurted out to the astonishment of my friends.

Lilly Mae licked her lips and looked at me for a long while before saying, "Well, it appears you have some cat in you yet, Carl. OK, I'm going to tell you how to catch a giant mouse. Here's the plan..."

5

The Replacement Kitty

Have you ever had "one of those days"? My day started off quite well and then I put my paw right into my mouth. I had to go and open up my mouth and get my friends all riled up. I felt I had to counter the bruising to my ego and accept Lilly Mae's plan... Lilly Mae's crazy, crazy plan.

You see, Lilly Mae had been plotting for years to go find Marvin and Mary Mouse but she didn't think a cat as large as her was in any shape for such a journey. She was content being the mastermind behind the operation and letting others have the glory of putting an end to the reign of the giant mice. I was a little concerned because, after all was said and done, I really didn't have much in the way of hunting experience. I was beginning to think that I would just cross my paws and hope that this would pass. Maybe the humans would simply forget about their vacation and Marvin Mouse. I couldn't have been more wrong.

Over the next few days, I watched the humans pack their bags and I overheard numerous conversations pertaining to Marvin Mouse.

"I can't wait to hug Marvin."

"I want Marvin and Mary mouse dolls."

"Mom, do you think we can have a picture with Marvin?"

"Mom, I want to stay in Mouse World forever!"

Mouse ears? Mouse World? Mouse Dolls? Pictures of Mice? Are these people out of their minds? Never once did I hear anyone even mention me. How am I supposed to eat without my servants here? Who will change my litter box? I look around and I don't see any pictures of myself or any cat dolls or any cat ears. These humans had no intention of forgetting their trip and in fact it seemed like they were actually getting more excited about it. I thought things couldn't get any lower when I heard the human female say, "Aunt Patricia said she would be happy to watch Carl for us while we are gone."

Aunt Patricia? No, this will not do. Why don't they just throw me in the dog pound? Aunt Patricia always likes to pick me up and kiss me on the head. She eats lots of horrible fruits and vegetables and never hears my cries for tuna or chicken. She has a little chubby terrier named Bella that likes to bark and threaten me while I'm trying to nap. She even goes and buries things in my litter box. This just won't do. I have to spend a week being kissed, starved, and barked at while my humans are on vacation spending all of their money on a giant rodent. What is wrong with the world these days?

I began to think of the plan that Lilly Mae presented to us. She said the outside cats didn't need to worry about covering their tracks since their owners would just say they "were out hunting." For me, things might be a little problematic. Aunt Patricia would surely know that I was missing and undoubtedly a panic would erupt. A part of me was tempted to ignite such a panic and teach the humans a valuable lesson, but another part of me didn't want to deal with a crisis. I could come back and find that I was replaced with some cute kitten or worse, a puppy. Lilly Mae said I would need to find a replacement cat, but I wasn't exactly sure how to go about doing it. The plan was on hold until such a replacement emerged.

I rummaged through all of the stuffed animals that the human children had accumulated over the years and, while I did find some lion and tiger animals, I didn't think that Aunt Patricia would fall for the ruse. Sure, one might say, I am essentially a lion or tiger, but when she noticed the stuffed animal wasn't eating, she would surely get suspicious. Suddenly, it dawned on me that the one who could replace me was a good friend of mine. I quickly ran to the window and began to call for Mars.

Mars and I are both brown tabbies, so it should be easy to pull off the masquerade. Mars is a little leaner than myself, but Aunt Patricia will still think she is kissing her favorite "fat cat." I was a little worried about Mars and his rather zany personality, but I'm sure Aunt Patricia will just look in a book and write it off as the "cat crazies." There is the little matter of her terrier, but maybe that's something I'll just leave to surprise Mars. Convincing Mars might be hard, so I will highlight the advantages of being a house cat.

I heard a low meow and turned to see Mars on the window sill looking at me with a curious expression.

"So, what is it Carl? Have you decided to go find the giant mouse?"

I nodded my head and then told him about the great opportunity I was offering him. "Mars, old buddy, old pal...how would you like to take a little vacation?"

"Vacation? Well, if I go on the mouse hunt, that's a vacation."

I cocked my head to one side and made my push. "The mouse hunt is more of a business trip you might say. It's not really a vacation, Mars. You see, I was thinking that you could vacation here for awhile."

Mars looked suspicious. "What do you mean here?"

"You would become me. It's kind of like a fantasy vacation. You would get treated like me and even called by my name. You would receive around-the-clock love and care and you would be fed at regular times," I tried my hardest to make the sell.

"Well, I don't know. I mean, I kind of wanted a part in the mouse hunt," Mars said with some hesitation.

"I didn't even tell you the best part, old buddy. You get to use my litter box and the humans will clean it." I figured this would get him, as every cat loves the fact that the humans have to clean up after us.

"Litter box huh? Well that does make it like a vacation, actually like a first class vacation. Yes, yes, I will become you!" Mars said while licking his lips. Yes, litter boxes are a big deal.

OK, I had my replacement, now I had to figure out where exactly Marvin Mouse's home was and how my group would get there.

6

Travel Arrangements

Travel arrangements are hard to make for cats. Sure, there are times that we are stuffed into a box or pet carrier and taken to be tortured by the veterinarian or, on occasion, taken on a trip. For the most part, though, we resist the human ways of travel. Such travel restricts our freedom and our ability to take care of cat business like hunting, eating, and sleeping. For this mission, it would be necessary to use some sort of human means of travel and to be honest; I didn't know how to go about arranging it.

"Carl, I hope you know that this isn't going to be easy," Rex said to start the meeting.

Cindy followed, "Don't be ridiculous, Rex, we're cats. We can do anything."

"I know, I know...it's just that I think we have to travel pretty far to get these mice and then we will still have to figure out how to get back home. We live in a town

40

called Indianapolis and Marvin Mouse is in a town called Houston. Jarvis, the three-legged poodle who lives near me, said it's a complete day and night to get there and back. It's not going to be a walk in the park," Rex said.

I began to pace on the kitchen table that was holding our meeting and contemplated calling off the whole thing. A complete day and night there and back must mean using the human car and since I have yet to see a cat drive, I would guess that idea was out of the question. I know the humans often say they fly, but I've never seen a human with wings, so I'm not sure how that works. The distance and the prospect of combating a couple giant mice seemed insane to me, but the idea of living in a household that bows down to that same mouse made me sick. Plus, house cat or not, it is every feline's desire to catch a big mouse. There were none bigger than Marvin.

"Rex, we have to find a way. The humans can drive, but we can't. The humans say they fly, but we can't. The humans always figure out a way to go to far away places, but we never do. Our Egyptian forefathers would never put up with this. We are letting the humans do whatever they like and, due to our laziness, they are starting to praise mice. This is insanity. We have to go and we have to go now!" I surprised myself with the intensity of my speech.

"He's right Rex, we have to go now. It's a matter of principle," Cindy said, eyeing Rex.

"OK, OK, I never said I wouldn't go. I guess there is a way, but it won't be comfortable. In fact, it might be miserable," Rex said with some resignation.

Cindy and I look at one another and back at Rex.

Rex continued, "Carl... your humans have that big motorhome thing that they travel in, right?" I nodded and he went on, "Well, we simply need to be on top of it when they leave on their trip."

I was briefly excited, "Great job, Rex. I knew you would come up with something…wait a second… did you say on top of it?"

The next few days were spent listening to the humans and then reporting my findings to my friends. Mars would have to be ready to move in as soon as Aunt Patricia arrived and the rest of us would have to be ready to board the motorhome. Rex and Cindy would be OK, as their humans would just think they were out hunting or exploring. I didn't like the idea of riding on top of the motorhome, but it was better than not being able to go at all.

One evening while I was lying under the human adult bed, I overhead the male say the magic words, "Honey, I guess we'll pull out at dawn the day after tomorrow."

"Sounds good to me, honey, let's plan on it. We'll be on the road by 7am."

So, there it was. They were leaving the day after tomorrow. I would have to have Mars in place by then and the rest of the crew on top of the motorhome. The humans were capable of changing plans, but on this matter I think they meant business.

The next day, I saw all of them packing and there was a sense of excitement in the air. On occasion, the human female would stop and look down at me and say something like, "I think he knows we're going somewhere" or "Hopefully, C-A-R-L doesn't know we're G-O-I-N-G tomorrow." I just looked up and dutifully meowed, but my insides were churning. They churned a little more when I saw the human female look out the window and say, "Aunt Patricia is here."

I moved like a deer to the window and began to meow. Mars needed to get here fast and assume his role. Aunt Patricia's terrier Bella would smell me and get my scent and then freak out when she realized a switch has been pulled. She might make life miserable for poor Mars and cause a lot of confusion and panic. I need her to smell Mars right from the start.

The human female moved to the front door to let Aunt Patricia in and I could hear the pitter patter of the hyper terrier's little feet. The crazy thing would jump on everyone and then make its move towards me. I had to find Mars fast. I let out another big meow, as the humans were too preoccupied with Aunt Patricia to pay much attention. *Where in the world is that crazy Mars?*

After the door opened and everyone was hugging one another and I caught a glimpse of the terrier as she tried to jump up on one of the girls. They were petting Bella and, while the little dog seemed content, I could see that crazy nose of hers moving. She was trying to lock in on to my scent. *Mars please, for the love of tuna, hurry up.*

I meowed again, knowing full well Bella would hear me, but I was panicking. I thought I heard a response

45

meow from far off, but it didn't matter. I could feel the cold wet nose of Bella pressing against me.

"Get away from me, mutt!" I yelled at the little pest.

"Mutt? Mutt? I'll have you know that I am a purebred," Bella answered smugly.

"You are a hyper, panting, smelly little mutt and if you keep sticking that cold nose in my face I'll swat it off," I said as I tried to keep her from memorizing my scent.

"I don't know why you insult me. I just want to play. I won't hurt you." Bella said.

After one more look out the window, I decided I would swallow hard and move to Plan B. I was going to use kindness and try to reason with this annoying creature.

"Look, Bella… I've had a long night. It's not easy to chase mice all day and so, I'm sorry if I'm coming off as a little rude." If my friends had heard me apologize to a dog, they would never let me live it down.

"You chase mice? That's funny, Carl. You're a funny cat. Everyone knows that all you do is just eat and sleep." The little terrier seemed happy to have the chance to take advantage of my kindness.

I made my tail stop moving so I didn't give away my increasing anger, but the little dog persisted.

"Carl, I'm pretty sure that if there is any mouse to catch around here, it will only be caught by a trap or your human's broom." Bella really seemed happy with herself and even gave me a playful nip on my leg.

I kept my claws sheathed and decided that an honest approach might appeal to Bella. After all, most dogs are loyal and hungry for friends. She might appreciate doing something for her old friend Carl.

"Bella, I want to ask you something. It's something that I wouldn't trust with just anyone, but since we are such good friends, I thought I could trust you." I said it, hoping I didn't come off as fake.

"I'm listening, Carl, old buddy, old pal."

"Well I'm going to take a little vacation, but it's a top secret vacation."

"Top secret vacation? I'm not sure I'm following," Bella said with her ears up and with obvious interest.

"Well, I need to take care of something. It's something that wouldn't concern a dog necessarily, but I assure you that it concerns a cat. You see, if I don't take care of this little situation, things might get a little dicey for me around here." I knew I was risking confusing the little mutt, but to her credit she hung in there.

"So, you need to go somewhere top secret and take care of something top secret? Well, if that's the case, I guess I can understand why you don't want a lot of people to know," Bella said with her little stub wagging away.

"Yeah, you see, you get it. Now, I'm leaving first thing in the morning. I'll be going with a number of friends and in fact, one of my friends will be staying here and masquerading as me." I dropped the bomb and awaited her response.

Bella cocked her head to her side while she processed things. Undoubtedly, she envisioned a number of cats coming over and a strange cat moving around in my place. Every instinct in her body was probably screaming out that she should do her duty as a dog and start barking and biting like crazy. Bella finally spoke up, "I think I can deal with everything but the part about your friend masquerading as you."

"Look, it'll be good for you. He's a nice cat named Mars. In fact, he's nothing like me at all, as he'll treat you with respect and play with you all the time." I was imploring Bella to go along with things, but she seemed to be distant.

"Carl, I have to give you your space since this is your territory and since my human has promised me lots of treats if I behave around you, but it goes against the whole dog and cat dynamic if I treat a strange cat nicely. No offense, Carl, but I'm going to have to freak out when I see your friend. It's a matter of principle." I had to hand it to Bella, as she was an honest and direct young dog.

"OK, you leave me no choice, Bella. What will it take for you to treat my friend nicely?" I hated to bargain with a dog, but I had no choice.

"Well, I want to be able to eat your food whenever I come over."

I grimaced, "Fine."

Bella wasn't finished, "I want you to play with me whenever I want."

I didn't like this part, as terriers had endless supplies of energy, "Fine."

Bella thought for a second and continued, "I want to be able to sleep in your bed whenever I'm here."

"OK, no problem, now, do we have a deal?" I wanted to end this little game fast.

"Well, there is one more thing…"

"Anything, name it and we're done." I was growing increasingly impatient.

"It gets cold out here, so I want to be able to use your litter box."

I was beginning to think that a world dominated by Marvin Mouse might not be the worst thing in the world.

7

Departure

The engine fired up on the motorhome and I began to puff out my fur in anticipation of the long and possibly cold ride. Rex and Cindy were both there and seemed eager for the adventure. Mars couldn't come to the window since he was being chased by Bella. I told him that if she ever caught him, just break out the claws and swat away. The poor guy was in for long ordeal. Despite my agreement with Bella, she still felt that non-stop playing with the cat had to take place. At this point, I was done arguing.

"Well, this is it. We're on the road!" Rex said with enthusiasm.

I have to admit it kind of bothered me that they couldn't tell the difference between Mars and me. Cindy said they're just excited about the trip and I told her that they need to get "unexcited" fast. A cat can only put up with so much nonsense.

I was a little scared when we began to move and I took a longing look back at the only home I can ever remember having. Oh sure, I was born in a box with a dirty towel like all the rest of us, but at some point, like all cats, I had left my litter. Rex believes it has to be this way or we'll end up fighting our mother and siblings for food. As I alluded to earlier, some cats get lucky and find homes where their servants, I mean humans, treat them right and some don't. Rex, Cindy, and Mars had nice owners but they were sometimes indifferent to their needs. My humans always made sure I had food and water. If a mouse, giant or not, wants to interfere with this, then it will have to deal with me.

The first part of the trip wasn't bad as we laughed and joked before taking a short nap. I wouldn't say it was the most comfortable ride in the world, but it was a means to an end. There were a few close calls as one time another motorist spotted Cindy leaning over the railing and almost drove off the road. They shadowed our vehicle for some time honking and pointing to the roof, but eventually they gave up. The human male probably thought they were crazy and the human female was likely sleeping.

Now you would think that a cat would be starving within minutes of such a trip and you would be right, but cats are also excellent at improvising. We aren't above a high protein bug meal and indulged all along the way. The act of swatting down a bug as it flew by me made my hunting instincts go wild. I was starting to feel like a real predator.

Hunter or not, I didn't like the periods of foul weather that we encountered along the way. We would go from blazing hot to a torrent of wind and rain in a matter of minutes. Rex didn't seem to mind all that much, but poor Cindy would just get her coat all shiny again when the motorhome would encounter another big downpour.

"I hope this crazy mouse is worth it. I'm starting to feel like a stinky wet dog!" Cindy moaned.

There were times during the trip that I had the chance to reflect on my life and it began to dawn on me how much it hurt to be out of my comfort zone and out of the thoughts of the human children. Despite the fact that we are solitary creatures at times, we still need love and praise like everyone else. My human children used to always compliment me on my beauty, but lately they seem to be interested in other things. Lately, they seem to be interested in mice. Where did I go wrong?

"Rex, are you sleeping?" I knew full well that he was, but I was in need of some cat to cat advice.

"Well I was sleeping, but I'm not right now," he said as his tail wagged furiously. I'm sure he wanted to swat me off the top of the moving vehicle, but he kept his cool.

"Look, I can't talk to Cindy about this, but I need to know from my best friend if what I'm doing is right or if I'm just doing it because I'm a paranoid cat."

"You're paranoid," Rex said, not wasting even a second to respond.

"Well, I was kind of hoping you might give it a little consideration."

Rex shook his head and explained, "It's not that I disagree with what you're doing at all. I mean, I'm here aren't I? I just think you sometimes fail to see what you have."

"What I have? What do I have? My humans don't treat me the same anymore. They barely acknowledge me and now I see them turning their attention to some crazy mouse. I mean for all I know they might be getting ready to replace me. Maybe I'm on the way out, while the mutant mouse is on the way in." After the words left my mouth, I realized that Rex was correct in calling me paranoid.

"Look, don't get all bent out of shape about it. You're one of the lucky cats and you just don't realize it. I don't blame you. You've only known the good life and now when there is a little adversity, you get a little nutso."

"What do you mean that I've only known the good life? Come on, I'm a cat. Cats have it tough no matter what we do," I protested.

"Tough? Forgive me pal, but you don't know what tough is. Cindy, Mars, and I have it far tougher than you and we still have it pretty easy. You, my friend, have it made."

I was a little confused. How in the world could my best friend say he has it easier than I do? I have to get up every day and go to my dish for a snack. The humans should be bringing me my food. I spend a great deal of time every day giving myself long baths so that my coat can be beautiful and the humans can admire it. Quite simply, it's not easy being me.

"Carl, you live the life all cats dream about having. Sure, we tell everyone we wish we were on the plains of Africa hunting zebras with the lions, but we all know that's just a story. We all want what you have quite frankly," Rex said it and suddenly I felt extremely guilty.

Rex continued, "Carl, you have a family. Your family lets you live in their home. You get to stay cool when it's hot out and warm when it's cold. You never experience rain or snow. You don't have to worry about fighting and you never have to run from an angry dog. Sure you have to put up with Bella on occasion, but that's nothing. You get three square meals a day no matter what and your litter box is always tended to in a timely manner. The rest of us? Well, it's not so great. I mean we all have humans who care about us at some level, but they rarely pick us up or spend any significant time with us. You get picked up and hugged and kissed all the time. Poor Mars hasn't been picked up since he was a kitten. In fact, none of us have been treated the same since we grew up. You, my friend, hit the jackpot."

The jackpot? I never really thought of it like that. I guess compared to my friends I did have it pretty good.

"Carl, you've never visited the dumpsters behind the grocery store or the garbage cans that fill the alleys. Yeah, I know, we all glamorize it, but it's not that great. No one likes to have to scavenge for an old piece of crust or a stinky bone. You get nice table scraps and little gourmet wet meals. Your dry food has all kinds of vitamins in each bite. I'm not trying to sound like a complainer, but the rest of us just aren't as lucky as you. Maybe it's time you take a little self-inventory, old buddy."

I didn't have much to say in reply. Rex was right. I had taken my life for granted and only now when it feels threatened do I even start to realize it. I curled into a ball and continued to think about everything Rex had told me. I was just starting to drift off to sleep when I felt the motorhome come to a stop.

8

The Pit Bull

Rex and Cindy watched as the humans departed their motorhome and walked into a nearby restaurant. I was still a little ashamed of my conversation with Rex, but shame would wait as I had some hunger pains that needed to be alleviated soon.

"The smell here is driving me crazy," Cindy said, as Rex and I nodded in agreement.

Rex smelled the sweet aroma of hamburger coming from the restaurant and began to lick his lips, "We have to get some of that food. I'm starving here."

"I'm in total agreement, but just how do you think we should go about it? Should we just walk in and meow an order of cheeseburgers?" Cindy was being a little smart-alecky, but I didn't care as my stomach was going crazy.

"Well, Carl, old buddy, I think you're going to get your first shot at a dumpster dive," Rex said with some cheer.

The three of us jumped down to a nearby truck and from there to the ground. Cats are a lot like humans in that they lose all patience when they get hungry. I had lost my patience some time ago and if climbing around in a dumpster meant I could get a meal in my belly, I was all for it.

As we rounded the restaurant and followed our nose to the dumpster, I could have sworn that I heard a bark. Yes, I said a bark. Now unless they do things a little different in this town, a bark usually means that a dog is nearby. Despite being hungry, I didn't want to have to deal with a dog at this point. Then I heard it again. *Bark.*

Cindy froze and looked at Rex who was looking at me.

I was the first to offer something, "Was it me, or did that bark sound really close?"

Bark. Bark.

Twice and really close.

"Rex, Cindy, there's the dumpster, run for it!" I yelled out and was already bouncing like a scared deer. All three of us jumped into the dumpster as we heard the movement of padded feet and the frantic sniffing of what was undoubtedly a dog's nose.

Rex whispered, "Let's all just stay very quiet and he'll probably go away."

Unfortunately, Rex was answered, "No, I won't go away. I know you three cats think you can outsmart me, but it won't happen. This is my territory and by extension, this is my dumpster. You're trespassing and I don't like it."

"Well, we don't care what you like, you mutt!" Cindy yelled out. Rex and I both winced because that would undoubtedly antagonize our pursuer.

"Mutt? Ha ha, you're a mouthy one. I didn't know pit bulls were mutts."

I swallowed hard when he identified himself as a pit bull. I began to think that negotiation might work. I mean it worked with Bella, surely it would work with some pea brained pit bull. I climbed to the top of the dumpster and looked down at what can only be described as a vicious monster. The pit bull had his upper lip curled back and snarled with a ferocity that almost made me faint.

"Have you given up already, cat?" the proud beast asked.

"Give up? No, not exactly. You see, we just need to get back to our humans. If you let us do that, we will promise to never put our paws on your territory again." I thought it sounded reasonable.

"Oh, so you're a big negotiator, huh? Cat, you are either very dumb or very brave. Pit bulls don't negotiate, we exterminate." The pit bull was growling and drooling and I have to admit, I was shaking.

"Well, I think I can speak for my friends when I say, we don't feel like being exterminated Mr. Pit Bull. I don't see how that will help anyone. How about this? How about if I find some nice tasty garbage in here for you? Would that be enough for you to let us go?"

The pit bull looked at me for a long while and started to pace. "Garbage? You're an interesting cat. The human who owns this restaurant will give me a nice tasty soup bone if I deal with garbage cats like you. But I'm reasonable: I might make things a little less painful if you tell me why you're here in the first place. You don't have the smell of a street cat. You smell like a house cat. Why would a house cat be rummaging around in my territory?"

"You might as well tell him," Rex whispered to me from inside the dumpster. Cindy didn't seem to mind as I noticed she had found something tasty to munch on. Even in a crisis, a cat can eat.

"Well, I know you're a busy dog, Mr. Pit Bull, so I'll get right to the point. You see we are on a quest to capture a giant mouse." I said it with a straight face, yet the wide eyed expression of the pit bull seemed to suggest I had said something insane.

"A giant mouse? Ha ha, you are an interesting cat. If you want a giant mouse, I would suggest you go find a skunk or ferret. A giant mouse? I think you're a giant goofball. There is no such thing as a giant mouse. I think kitty cat has been munching on the catnip too long." The pit bull was happy with his insults and seemed to relax a little bit.

"I'm glad you find it funny, but I can assure you it is true." I said with a little more conviction.

The pit bull sat down and appeared to be thinking. He seemed a little confused. "Cat, by any chance are you talking about Marvin Mouse?"

I froze and looked down at my wide eyed partners. "How do you know about Marvin Mouse?"

"Well, a long time ago one of the human boys in the house started walking around with a mouse mask on. I thought I was losing my mind. The next thing I know I see him wearing shirts with a mouse on it and singing songs about a mouse named Marvin. Needless to say, I was a little disturbed. One day, I noticed he had a Marvin Mouse blanket and even a lamp that resembled a mouse," the pit bull said.

"I think I'm going to be sick," I told him.

"Cat, tell your friends to come out of there. I won't hurt any of you," the pit bull told me without a hint of anger in him anymore.

The three of us jumped to the ground and took a seat near our former foe. Cindy even rubbed against him as he suddenly seemed saddened.

"What happened to your human boy?" Cindy asked.

"He changed. He was into all of this mice garbage and basically forgot about me. It was a bad time for me. The boy found other interests and I've been largely ignored ever since. I always told myself that someday I was going to go to his little Mouse World and put a good bite into Marvin, but it seems like I'm always busy guarding my territory."

"Come with us," I blurted out. Rex gave me an icy stare, but I didn't care. I hadn't thought about the problem of getting a pit bull on top of the motor home or what would happen to him following the mission.

"Me? Come with a bunch of cats? Yeah, right. I guess I could use a vacation and yeah, I would like to confront Marvin, but hanging with you three could hurt my reputation," the pit bull said as if he was torn.

"Oh come on, you guard a dumpster for crying out loud. What reputation?" Rex was playing with fire with such words but it seemed to strike a chord with the pit bull. I think Rex suddenly saw the wisdom in having this ferocious beast with us and was challenging the dog's pride. Seriously, who would mess with a pit bull?

"You know, you're right. I'm in."

Cindy was the first to give him a congratulatory head butt. Suddenly, I realized we didn't even know his name.

"I'm Carl and this is Rex and this lovely lady is Cindy."

"Well, it's nice to meet all of you. I'm sorry I was going to eat you a little earlier."

We looked at one another and just nodded that the apology was accepted.

The pit bull stared at my best friend and said, "Rex, huh? That's a dog name, ya know."

"Someone told me that once or a thousand times," Rex said as he looked at me.

"What's your name anyway?" Cindy asked.

"Tab, it's short for Tabby," he said without the slightest indication that he had a cat name.

Rex started to say something but I shook my head. No, it was better not to get this alliance off on the wrong foot.

We made our way back to the parking area and quickly noticed that there was a major problem. The motorhome was gone.

9

Strange Hitchhikers

I was beginning to think that we had reached the end of the road. We were stranded in a strange town somewhere between our homes and the home of Marvin Mouse. At least, that was my guess, as it was turning dark and we had traveled all day. If it was a complete day and night from my home to Marvin's, then halfway sounded reasonable.

Tab was leading us out of town and we took him at his word that he knew the way to Houston. If there is one thing I have to give a dog, it's that they are usually good with directions. Our attitudes were in decline as we were all hungry, thirsty, and cold. I made it a point not to complain, as I wanted to be strong next to my outdoor friends. However, I have to admit, I was miserable.

"How much further is it?" Cindy asked and even though I winced at the question, I was wondering as well.

"I won't lie to you crazy cats; we still have a long way to go. Our pads will be worn out by the time we get there," Tab said to the collective groan of the group.

"Let's hitch a ride," Rex blurted out.

"Two problems with that… one, we don't have thumbs and two, we can't tell the human driver where to take us," Tab seemed to put an end to Rex's idea with his two excellent points.

Rex nodded and dutifully trudged on. It was at that moment the rain started and I began to think of the lunacy of the situation. Three cats and one dog marching down the side of a freeway in the pouring rain in an effort to catch a giant mouse. If it wasn't so silly, I would cry.

My fur was soon soaking wet and flattened against my skin. For one of the first times, I was wishing I was a human and had one of their automobiles. I was also wishing that we hadn't left the motorhome. The whole operation seemed to be going up in smoke. I could hear

Cindy grumbling and one look at Rex betrayed his poor mood. Tab seemed to be upbeat. I thought that he must be still beaming from being included in our adventure. It was at that point that one of the passing vehicles slowed down and pulled over on our side of the road.

Rex, Cindy, and I quickly moved behind Tab. He put his head down and showed his teeth. He was growling and making it clear to whoever was in the car that he was not to be messed with. The car door opened and an arm reached out holding what looked to be part of a hamburger. Tab stiffened and his nose went wild. All of a sudden his tail started to wag and he abandoned us for the tasty hamburger.

"He goes from protecting us one minute to devouring a hamburger the next. So much for loyalty," Cindy said sadly. I'm not sure if she was more disappointed in Tab or the fact she didn't get any hamburger.

An elderly and slightly portly woman emerged from the car and gave the satisfied Tab a pat on the head. She looked at us with a pleasant smile and gave the standard human, "Here kitty, kitty, kitty..." Normally I would ignore this insult, but I was wet, hungry, and tired and started to run towards her. I noticed Rex and Cindy were right behind me.

She gave each of us some warm French fries from her sack and gave us the reassuring "nice kitty" compliment. I'm not normally a potato eater, but I can, honestly say, these tasted wonderful.

"You are all such nice animals, why are you out here in this foul weather?" She was genuinely concerned for us, but since the humans haven't mastered the animal language and since we choose not to speak the human tongue, there was a definite language barrier.

Tab turned and motioned us to get in the car. I wasn't sure it was the best idea in the world, but since the rest of the group was willing, I followed them. The warm car was much more preferable than the wet ground.

The human woman climbed in the car and looked us over again. "Well, I'm not sure what to do with you tonight. I'm sure you have owners and they're probably worried sick, but there would be no way to find them tonight. I guess you're stuck with me. But don't you worry: I'll dry you off and fatten you up."

Tab turned to us and said, "I know this is a hiccup in our plan, but let's dry off and eat some food. We'll deal with things tomorrow."

We all nodded in agreement and huddled together in the back seat. The older woman hummed as she drove up to the side of her small home. She turned to us and smiled, "Well, this is my home sweet home. Please come and join me." We all jumped out of the car and followed her to the front door.

I was only one paw into her home when I smelled it. I smelled the air and noticed Rex and Cindy were doing the same. Tab was too anxious for food to stop and take a whiff of the air, but we were all very aware of what was in the home with us. To be honest, I heard it before I actually saw it.

"Squawk! Why are you cats in my home? Squawk!"

I turned and saw a giant multi colored parrot looking down at me. This night was getting more depressing every second.

"I don't know if I'm looking at a future friend or a future meal," Rex said as he eyed the large parrot.

"I'm thinking friend. I'm not sure if I want to tangle with that guy and his large beak," Cindy said. I kept my mouth shut, but I agreed with Cindy. Some birds are simply better left alone.

"Squawk! A future meal? Ha ha, I'll make you into a cat barbeque if you keep eyeing me that way! Squawk!"

The parrot either had a strange sense of humor or that was a definite threat.

"OK, OK, I'm sorry. I just wasn't expecting to see a giant bird," Rex said as he looked up at the parrot.

"Squawk! You weren't expecting to see a giant bird? Well, do you think I was waiting around all day to see a wet dog and three cats come walking into my territory? Squawk!" The parrot had a point. This whole thing was getting odder by the moment.

Our rescuer came and started putting down bowls of water and plates of table scraps for us to devour. We all left our conversation with the parrot to dive into our bounty.

The meal was wonderful. We all enjoyed stew with lots of meat and sauce. I thought Tab would eat his bowl as well since he acted so hungry. Being that we are like most animals and have bottomless stomachs, we wanted more, so we really let our host have it with some loud begging. High pitched meows filled the room and our host was soon digging through her cupboard to give us some tuna and milk. Tab was given the additional bonus of some cheese.

We all lay down and relaxed with a quick shower. I was washing my face with one of my paws when Cindy asked an important question, "So, what now?"

I was going to answer her with an "I don't know" when I heard the old lady on the phone.

"You won't believe it but I found the sweetest dog and three adorable cats. Yes, I agree, my parrot takes up most of my time. Yes, yes... I agree, the animal shelter would be the perfect place for them."

Cindy looked at Rex, who looked at me, and I, in turn, looked at Tab.

"What's an animal shelter?" I asked.

Tab looked horrified and answered, "It's an animal prison."

I started to feel faint. The world turned to black.

10

Captured

As soon as our host retired to her bedroom, we all went to confront her parrot. While I am not overly fond of birds, I have to admit their willingness to speak the human language could be advantageous. There are many pluses to saying "food" instead of "meow". Try as we might, we can't get the humans to always understand the various tones of our beautiful meowing. They just aren't smart enough. A parrot can specify what they want and not have to play the silly human games. Of course we could too, but we have way to much pride.

Tab was the first to start in on our feathered host, "Listen bird, we need you to talk some sense into your owner. We don't have time to go to prison. We need to get to Mouse World and fast."

"Squawk! First of all my name is Tango. Second of all, your little mission is exactly that, your little mission. If you end up in prison along the way, that's your problem. Squawk!"

Tab eyed the parrot and was probably calculating if a strong jump would give him a shot to catch him, but the seriousness of the situation prevailed. Tab took a breath and tried some good old fashioned kindness.

"Tango, I didn't mean any disrespect. I was just thinking that maybe you could tell your owner that instead of taking us to prison, that she could take us to Mouse World instead. What do you say, old buddy?" Tab even wagged his tail for effect, but Tango would have none of it.

"Squawk! First off, we aren't old buddies. Second off, I think it's kind of funny that your little vacation is going to be interrupted by a stay in the old clink. Squawk!"

Tab's eyes widened and he started to growl, "I don't find the humor in being put in a cell. I will tell you what I find funny though and that is the fact that you have a cat standing right behind you."

Tango turned to see Rex staring him right in the face. Rex had climbed and jumped like the expert hunter he is, until he was sitting on some shelving that sat right across from Tango's perch.

Rex smiled, "Don't try flying because I'll be on you before the first wing flaps."

Tango was trapped and had no choice but to enter into negotiation. "Squawk! This is humiliating! Squawk!"

Tango and Rex both jumped down to the floor. We immediately pressed the parrot to squawk some sense into his owner and to have her take us to Mouse World instead of the animal prison. Tab told us just how dire things could be if we were imprisoned, "None of you cats have any kind of tags on you. Unless you have a chip in you, you'll be put up for adoption. It'll be the same for me."

"Adoption? Well, that won't do. Not unless I'm adopted by a chicken farm owner," Cindy said in some alarm.

"We could end up in some pretty bad situations. It might be manageable for Cindy and me, but you could have owners that don't let you in the house," Rex said as he looked at me.

I was starting to digest the whole situation when Tab added another bleak bit of information. "Well you're all fairly young, so you might get lucky and find a home. I'm not a puppy anymore. I have some years on my paws and most humans don't appreciate that. I could get the sleeping shot."

"They give you a shot to help you sleep?" Cindy asked.

"Yeah, it helps you sleep, but the thing is, you don't wake up." Tab said grimly.

Don't wake up? What was this dog trying to say? My mind was racing and from the silence in the room, so were the minds of my friends.

"Squawk! That's not good. I might not care for you four, but I don't want to see you locked up or worse, sent off to night-night land. Squawk!" Tango's words made me feel a little better since it cemented our alliance.

"Tango, do you think your owner will listen to you?" I asked.

"Squawk! Oh, she'll listen to me, but it's the whole acting on what-I-say that worries me. Squawk!" Now, I was worried again.

Our human host woke up fairly early and began to work on some eggs that I quickly surmised were for our hungry stomachs. She was a good woman and fed us right, but her next few actions were of life and death importance. If Tango couldn't convince her to take us to Mouse World, we would have to attempt an escape and I hated the idea that we might have to scratch or bite the dear woman so that we could get away.

Despite the crisis in front of us, we all decided to indulge in the delicious scrambled eggs that were placed before us. Dogs and cats have hearty appetites and can eat basically any time. Even with Tango looking disgusted at our ability to devour eggs, I was in flavor heaven.

Tango put aside his anti-egg sentiments in an attempt to communicate to his human that she needed to rethink her plans.

"Squawk! Mouse World! Mouse World! Dogs, cats, Mouse World! Squawk!" Tango kept repeating himself and his human kept staring with wide eyes. Now, a parrot can never be as eloquent with a human as it is with other animals. For one thing, the humans will feel threatened by the animal's obvious higher intelligence and secondly, it would just disrupt the whole order of things. We let the humans feel superior, but all along they are doing our bidding. It's not a perfect system, but it works.

Tango's human kept listening and then suddenly shrugged her shoulders, went to the cupboard, and came back with a cracker for the parrot. Tango, like any animal, took time out from his cries to devour the tasty snack.

"Come on, Tango, keep talking to her," Rex pleaded.

"Squawk! I know what I'm doing, cat! She always thinks that when I talk, I must want some food. The sad thing is that I usually do. Squawk!"

"Bird, you better stop talking to us and get to talking to her. She's putting her shoes on!" Tab was alarmed and I could see he was tensing up. The moment of truth was undoubtedly at hand.

It was at that moment that the doorbell rang. Our host sighed and approached the door like she already knew who was behind it. She cracked the door open and began a conversation with whoever was on the other side. It sounded like there was more than one voice.

"I have a bad feeling about this," I whispered to my friends.

Our host turned to us and, in the usual nauseating voice humans use to talk to animals, she began calling to us, "Here kitty, kitty, kitty." Of course, we did what all self-respecting cats do and just sat there looking at her. If I don't see food, I don't run for "here kitty, kitty, kitty."

"Why is she acting like this?" Cindy asked.

The woman turned and opened the door and said, "It's no use. I feel bad about it, but we should try your plan."

"What plan?" I asked aloud and to no one in particular.

Tango looked nervous and flew up to his perch. "Squawk! I tried, I tried! Squawk!"

A man and woman appeared in the doorway. They both had matching uniforms on and were wearing gloves. Tango sniffed the air and informed us that they were sweating. They were nervous. This in turn made us nervous. Tango showed his teeth and began to growl and tensed up ready for a fight.

Our host turned to the two and said, "You better try your plan now, they're getting aggravated."

The young man nodded and reached into his bag and pulled out a large piece of red meat. "C'mon, puppy. C'mon and get your snack." Tab smelled, the growling ceased, and he started to wag his tail. Even with a full stomach, he was open to the human bribe.

As the three of us watched, Tab was led outside. I jumped up on the window sill and saw that he followed the meat to the back of a large truck. The human threw the meat in the back, Tab jumped in after the meat. The door was then promptly locked behind him.

"Rex! Cindy! Be careful, they're using bribery. They have Tab!" I screamed it out, but it was too late. The young female was holding pieces of tuna and my friends were hypnotized. The young man ran back with three little travel cages and placed them on the ground. Tuna was placed in two of them and Rex and Cindy quickly followed.

"I'll take care of this kitty," the young man said as he reached for me.

I swatted his hand and hissed and spit, but he just smiled. "It's OK kitty cat, I'm your friend."

He was, most assuredly, not my friend and if he stuck his hand in my face again he would learn what it felt like to be my enemy. Of course, he did to me what he did to my friends and it was game over. I smelled the tuna and it was like a magnet to my nose. My eyes glazed over and I felt my feet moving. I saw the tuna hit the floor of the travel cage and I pounced on it and quickly ate. It was at that point that I heard the door shut and I realized that I was done. I had been captured.

The humans knew that our stomachs were our weakness and they capitalized on it. We were all suddenly in deep, deep trouble.

11

Prison

I think that some humans believe that a cat or dog would find an animal shelter to be a fun place. They probably think that hearing a non-stop chorus of "meows" or "barks" would comfort us and provide us with a sense of family. They might think that having so many people tell us "good kitty" or "good puppy" would give us high self-esteem and make us praise every second of our time there. The fact of the matter is that they would be wrong and in fact, I would go so far as to say they are insane for even thinking it.

The humans call them animal shelters, but we call them prisons. Tab mentioned that the city has maximum security prisons called pounds and they must really be tough because I have yet to meet anyone who has escaped from one. I've met a few cats who have been paroled out of the animal shelter jails and they all say that being free on the outside is much more preferable than being locked up in those small cages. I now know how they feel since I'm currently in a cage.

The humans are basically nice and, in their typical human way, they think they're doing a good thing. I will say this for them, they are incredibly patient. Some of the dogs and cats here can get pretty crazy. In my first hour here, I saw one dog attempt an escape, another mistake a prison guard's leg for a fire hydrant, and yet another gave a guard a good chomp on his hind quarter. The humans seem to laugh it off and continue with their praise of us. I keep thinking that if they truly meant what they say, such as we are "good kitty cats" or "cutie pies" then they would reward us with fresh chicken or beef, but that just doesn't happen. They give us bland dry food. I eat it, of course, but just out of spite.

I couldn't see Rex or Cindy from my cage, nor could I hear them over the loud non-stop chorus of meows.

The noise in this prison is deafening. Cats call out for each other and their old humans, and they cry for more food. Sometimes they cry because they see new kittens getting paroled right away while they wait for someone to come and ask for them. It's quite sad and yet, I wasn't so naïve to think that I couldn't end up just like them.

The humans also have a little mean streak in them. I had only been in my cell for a few minutes when one of them opened it up and snatched me by the back of the neck and proceeded to place me in a wash tub. A wash tub? These humans have some nerve. I take between six and eight showers a day. How many do they take? I hissed and tried to escape but they held firm and covered me in barely warm water and some kind of smelly soap. It took me a good three hours to dry out and then another hour of showering myself to get the horrible smell to go away.

Just when I was beginning to settle down and take a nap, another human opened the cage and grabbed me behind the neck. Before I knew what was going on, I was on the receiving end of a series of shots. I tried my hardest to get away or to give them a good old fashioned bite, but they held me down and tried to tell me that "it was for my own good." I will remember to tell them that when I'm swatting away at them.

I sat and watched the endless procession of humans file by my cage. Some of them stopped to stare at me or to stick a finger in my cage. I considered biting them, but I just didn't have the energy. My friends were out of site and I was out of ideas. Even if I could get free, how would I help my friends escape? If I did get out of here, where would I go? My humans were undoubtedly in Mouse World right now and if I didn't get out of here soon and take care of Marvin Mouse, this whole thing will be an official disaster. It's possible that my humans could come home and even think Mars is me and never know the difference since they'll have on their little mouse blinders.

In that case, I would be lost forever. I have created quite a mess for myself.

There comes a time in every cat's life where they have to make some hard decisions. Sure, for some cats that might just be whether or not they sleep on top of the couch or on the human bed, but for me, the time had come for a life changing decision. Was I going to be the spoiled house cat that my friends knew or will I be a bold and inspirational cat? Bold wasn't just deciding to go on a trip to confront a mutant mouse with my friends. No, bold required taking a risk such as a jail break. I wanted to be bold. I wanted to make my lion and tiger cousins proud.

I had watched enough of the silly movies with which the humans rot their brains out to know that a little ruse can go a long way. I decided that I would put my acting skills to work and prove once in for all that cats are far superior to humans when it comes to intelligence.

I waited until one of the prison guards started walking toward my row of cages and then I rolled on my back, stuck my legs in the air, and slid my tongue out the side of my mouth. I was doing the old dog trick of "playing dead."

The prison guard almost did a double take when she saw me laying there. She bent over and started to study me. She was trying to determine if I was just sleeping in a strange position or if something more serious was wrong. I slowed my breathing to almost nothing and I froze into place.

"Kitty cat, wake up…kitty…," she said hesitantly. I could sense her nervousness. She tapped on the cage in an effort to startle me, but I stayed strong. Finally, she signaled to some of her fellow guards and shared a few whispers with them. I could hear them telling each other to be nonchalant around the public and to just pick up the entire cage and carry it to the back. They obviously didn't want any of the human shoppers to get alarmed.

The guards picked up my cage and silently took me to the room in the back where they had given me those horrible shots. One of the guards opened the cage and gently pulled me out and placed me on the bed. The lady, who had given me the shots, put an instrument up to my chest and started listening. She smiled and nodded and all of the guards let out their breath in relief.

"Well, he's breathing, but it's slow. He might be really depressed," the lady said with a smile. She turned to me, "Are you sick, kitty? Kitty cat sick?" Oh, if these humans only knew what they sounded like. I played along and let out a weak meow.

"You can all go back to work; I'll keep an eye on him in here. I just want to be sure nothing else is wrong with him," the lady said as she waved her hands to dismiss her co-workers.

The lady turned to me and said, "Well, little kitty cat, I guess you're stuck with me for awhile. You just relax. If you're really good, I'll give you a treat later."

You can sweet talk me all you like, but I'll never forget that shot you gave me. Well maybe for a whole chicken or tuna, but that's neither here nor there.

The lady sat down at a desk and began reviewing some papers. These humans with all of their papers, books, and computers are so depressing. They never take time to enjoy the good things in life such as a good piece of fish and lots of attention to their cats. If there are two things that humans love more than the items I just mentioned, those are their televisions and phones. I was counting on one of them to provide a distraction to this woman very soon. As soon as I thought about it, I heard the familiar ring of a phone. The lady reached into her coat pocket, smiled, and answered with a happy sounding "hello" to an obvious friend. Humans are so predictable.

I could tell she was just beginning a very lengthy conversation as she put her feet up on her desk and started talking about a previous day of shopping. Using all of my built in cat skills, I slinked off the table and ever so silently made my way across the room. The door had been left open a crack and I gently nudged it open a few more inches with my paw. I looked out and noticed that the guards were all busy talking to the shoppers or tending to other cats and dogs. This was my chance to find Rex, Cindy, and Tab.

"Meows" and other strange cries surrounded me as I made my way past every cage. I saw every kind of tabby imaginable, but I couldn't find my friends. "Cindy! Rex!" I called out, but heard no answer. I have to admit that the thought had crossed my mind that one of the human shoppers had bought them, but I couldn't imagine that Rex or Cindy would go willingly. Well, maybe Cindy would if she was bribed with some fish or chicken. The humans had mastered the art of bribery when it came to animals.

Many of the cats I passed were in shock to see me walking freely and they started to ask questions that I was sure would get me recaptured.

"Hey, how did you get out?"

"Hey, take me with you fella!"

"Tell the world my story."

I wish I could have taken all of them with me, but there is no way I could get all of the cages open and ensure their freedom. I wanted to tell them why I couldn't help, but I simply had no time. Suddenly, I saw Cindy and Rex. They were together and in some kind of twisted display room the humans had created. There were trees that cats were climbing on, boxes that cats were hiding in, and toys resembling mice scattered all around the room. Some of the cats were playing, but most were sitting and looking bored. It was essentially a cat exercise room and the human shoppers were allowed to come and watch them. I found the whole thing to be disturbing.

Rex and Cindy were both sitting in a corner with a look that I have heard described as "shell shocked." The poor things were probably shoved into this room with these strange cats without any warning. Throw in the fact that a human wave of gawkers always seemed to occupy the window and it would be easy to see how they could get rattled. I started to jump up and down hoping that none of the guards or wandering human shoppers would spot me. Fortunately, the crowds had died down a bit and there weren't enough eyes to catch me trying to get my friends attention.

Rex quickly spotted me and both he and Cindy ran to the window. "Get us out of here!"

I knew time was of the essence and therefore, a radical plan was necessary. I noticed that one of the trees the cats were allowed to climb on was thick and obviously heavy, while the viewing window was thin and somewhat flimsy. I studied for a second and then yelled my plan to

Cindy and Rex. I knew that we would be discovered any second so they had to act fast.

"Look, Mommy, a kitty cat is out of its cage." I heard a little girl a few yards away say the words and then there was a cascade of whispers as all of the humans noticed that I was loose. Cindy, Rex, and all of the cats in the room jumped on the tree and began to rock it. They used their amazing cat balance to get it to rock at a violent rate and then adjusted their weight so the tree would come crashing into the window. I scrambled out of the way as the window shattered into hundreds of pieces and a dozen cats came flying into the main room.

People screamed with fear and others laughed with joy as cats ran and jumped throughout the room. Security guards ran about trying to catch the animated cats. This diversion would serve us well. I chirped to my friends and motioned them to follow me. We turned a corner and scurried behind a large cat and dog cardboard display.

"That was really smart, Carl, good work," Rex said. I like compliments as much as the next cat, but this wasn't the time or place.

"Yes, thank you, Carl. I guess I was wrong about you. You are a smart cat," Cindy said. Normally I might be offended by a comment like that, but at this point it didn't matter. Any time an outside cat compliments a house cat, it's considered a big moment, but all I wanted to do at this particular moment was to get out of our current predicament.

"Before you start patting me on the back, we need to find Tab," I said and motioned to the dog area. I didn't want to head into a dog holding area for obvious reasons, but this wasn't the time to get wishy-washy.

We knew what we had to do and we knew we had to do it while there was all the commotion taking place in the cat area. As a unit, we ran into the dog area and set off a barking chorus like none of us could have ever imagined.

"Look, look, cats are here!"

"Get away cats; this is our part of the prison!"

"Come here kitty cat, I want to take a bite out of you."

The comments were terrible, but we trudged on and peered through every cage. I saw one elderly rat terrier and asked, "Excuse me sir, but you wouldn't happen to know a pit bull by the name of Tab would you?"

The rat terrier studied me for a moment and then his eyes seemed to bulge out of their sockets as he asked, "Are my eyes deceiving me or are you a cat?"

"Cat or dog, it's all apples and oranges right now. I need to find my friend Tab and I need to find him fast," I pleaded.

"Unbelievable. I didn't think I would ever see or smell a cat again. Oh, what I wouldn't do to give you a chase, but my poor old legs just can't move like they used to." The terrier seemed to be reliving some far away thought when he smiled and offered, "I'll make you a deal, kitty cat. I'll tell you where to find your friend if you let me out and allow me to chase you out of this place."

"Chase me out of here? What are you talking about, old timer?"

The terrier stood up and said in a whisper, "Look, I'm no spring chicken. I know I'm getting closer and closer to the great sleep. You see, if I can show that I'm worth something as a cat chaser, I'll see a big rise in my stock. I'll be the dog that saved the day."

I saw his point and would have, undoubtedly, done the same thing had I been walking with his paws. "Mr. Terrier, you have a deal," I said with a smile.

The rat terrier was true to his word and pointed to a holding area in the rear. I yelled at Rex and Cindy to move toward it and release the latch to the door so Tab could push it open. I had to keep my word and let the old timer out.

"Stretch your legs, Mr. Terrier, you're about to give chase one last time," I said. The terrier's bones cracked as he stretched. I could hear the security guards approaching and turned to see Rex and Cindy leading Tab back to my position.

"I didn't know you had it in you, Carl. Good work." Tab said. It's a great honor to be complimented by an outside cat, but it's not every day a pit bull compliments you. I could have basked in that all day long, but time was of the essence.

"OK folks, here come the guards!" Rex yelled out.

The security guards had nets and muzzles but they were still missing something. They didn't have the pure intelligence of a cat. I turned to the old timer and told him it was time to start the show. It took him a second to get his engine running and then he started to growl and run towards us. We all moved as one through the mass of guards with the old terrier in pursuit.

"Look at that dog go!" one of the guards yelled.

"He's even chasing a pit bull!"

The guards and the human shoppers seemed fixated on the old rat terrier that was single handedly chasing three full grown cats and a large pit bull. Tab ran ahead and snouted the handicap symbol and the doors opened. We bounded out, but not before I yelled back to the terrier, "Thank you, old timer. You were perfect."

"No, thank you, I heard someone say they wanted to adopt me. Yahoooooo…!" He barked with excitement as we bounded through the parking lot and into some nearby bushes. We were free.

12

The Parrot Surprise

Tab didn't waste any time in getting to the point. "OK, it was just a minor hiccup. Our intelligent friend Carl made sure the experience didn't get any worse. It happened and now we put it behind us. The mission to find Marvin Mouse hasn't changed. We put our heads down and our best paw forward."

The speech may not have been like how the human sport leaders address their teams, but it refocused our traumatized and ever-hungry minds. We had to get moving again, even if it was putting our pads through the pain of walking. I could tell from everyone's faces that doing the walking route again wasn't that appealing.

"Look...I got you all into this and while I have to see it through, I won't hold it against anyone if you want to turn back now. This is really my chore." I felt like I had to say it.

Rex swatted me and hissed, "Carl, old buddy, just when I was starting to think you're the smartest cat in the world you have to go and say something goofy. We're your friends and friends don't turn their back on friends."

Cindy continued, "We wanted this adventure. We wanted to support our friend. Plus, I have to admit, the chance to munch on a giant mouse makes this whole thing pretty appealing."

Tab laughed, "Well, I don't care about making the mouse into a sandwich, but I do want to see this through. Dogs aren't quitters and from what I've seen today, I guess cats aren't either. Carl, whether you like it or not, we're with you all the way. "

"Do you have any idea how we're going to get there?" I asked, already knowing the answer.

Tab sighed, "We do what we always do, use our paws."

I smiled a big toothy grin and looked towards the road. "Time is a wasting, let's go!" With that, we all bounded onto the side of the highway and began to make our way south toward Mouse World.

Our attitude was staying strong and our pace was fairly quick, but I have to admit my feet were getting sore. I wanted to ask Tab how far he might think we'd gone, but after I saw the snarl he gave Rex for asking the same question, I thought I had better hold my tongue.

We had to have been on the road at least an hour when I started to feel my legs burning. I figured if my legs were hurting than Rex and Cindy were either experiencing it as well or soon would be. Tab would undoubtedly last longer than us, but even he would have to stop for a rest pretty soon. It was around this time that a car slowed and stopped on the side of the road a few yards ahead of us. Having gone through this once before, I became instantly guarded and mentally prepared myself for what would come next. Would it be a potential friend or could it be someone from the prison?

Tab didn't waste any time in putting himself into a fighting position. "Get behind me cats. If this is an attempt to lock us back up, then I'll take them on. Once you start hearing my teeth snapping, just run for the bushes. Keep going south and you'll be fine."

"You're crazy if you think we're leaving you anywhere," Rex told the pit bull. "Sticking together doesn't just apply to cats: it applies to friends, period!"

"Ditto," Cindy and I said in unison. Tab had become a friend and we would stand by him no matter what transpired.

It was around this time that I thought I heard a strange noise. It sounded bird like, but I just couldn't be sure. The door to the car opened and dropping down to the ground was none other than the multi-colored parrot, Tango.

"Squawk! Can't I even get a hello out of this motley group? Squawk!" Tango said. I would say we trusted Tango, but it was his owner we were worried about. She was soon emerging from her car and following Tango to where our group stood.

"Oh, it is you! Look at you, poor things!" The human cried out, but whether she was sincere or setting us up for capture was still a question that needed answering.

"Parrot, if your human is planning on taking us back to prison, I need to warn you that things are about to get pretty ugly," Tab said as he growled.

"If she's here to take us to prison, than I can promise you that I'll be having some Tango Noodle Soup," Rex said as he went into his hunting stance.

"Squawk! Hold on, hold on, you ungrateful things. You don't have to get all bent out of shape. We're both here to help you. Squawk!" Tango said as he held up his wings.

Tango's human held up her arms as well and started to cry, "I am so sorry, my little friends. I didn't want to turn you over to the animal shelter, but I didn't know what else to do. I wanted you to go there so you could find nice homes and start fresh lives. I didn't know there was already a plan for you."

"Plan? What is she talking about?" I asked. How could a human possibly know our plan?

Tango looked at me and cackled, "Squawk! Cats are so small minded. I just told her what you had told me. You and your friends here wanted me to work on her and so I did. I wouldn't let her relax. I kept talking about cats, dogs, and Mouse World over and over again. I thought the poor thing would go crazy, but then suddenly the light bulb went on for her. She started to understand. Squawk!"

"I know everything, you poor little animals. You just want to go to Mouse World and see your masters," the human said with sincerity.

Cindy looked at me, "Masters? This lady needs her head examined."

"She can say whatever she wants, as long as she is on the up and up and plans on taking us to Mouse World," Rex added.

I was having a hard time believing that the "light bulb" just came on for this human, but I do know that birds can be annoying pests and that humans are easy prey for repetitive messages. I've watched the human male in my family become obsessed about a car or boat just because the sports programs he views constantly advertise such items. I guess this could also explain why my human children wanted to go to Mouse World so very badly. If it's told to them over and over again that this mouse is great, they start to believe it. Sometimes I truly pity these humans.

Tango's human attempted a peace offering and opened a package of hot dogs and offered each of us one.

Tab didn't waste any time and was on his third hot dog by the time I bit into my first. We might have still been a little leery of this woman, but we did have our stomachs to think of after all.

"You all eat and then go hop in my car. I'll have you to Mouse World in no time," the human told us.

Tab turned to us, "Guys, I kind of want to bite her as much as you probably do, but this is our ticket. Tango says it's cool and he knows what will happen if it's not. I say we do it."

Tango shrugged his wings and started moving towards the car, "Squawk! Leave it to a pit bull to imply violence! Here I am trying to do you a favor and this is my reward! Squawk!"

"We appreciate it, Tango. We really do. You worked some magic," I said. We loaded up into the car. It was quite a sight as we had a human driver, pit bull passenger, and a back seat with three cats and a parrot.

"I want you all to just relax and before you know it, we will be at Mouse World," the human said from the front seat.

We were a few miles down the road when Rex turned to Tango and asked what we were all wondering. "What exactly happened after we were taken away? How does a little parrot convince a human to become a cat and dog chauffer?"

Tango straightened up and seemed to relish the chance to tell his story. "Squawk! Well now the worm has turned. The parrot gets to educate the pit bull and the cats. I love it. Squawk!"

Rex gave him a gentle swat, "Don't push it."

"Squawk! All right, you maniac! Here's the story. My human was heartbroken when you all left. She was full of guilt and wondered aloud if she had done the right thing. I kept going crazy and saying over and over again that the cats need to get to Mouse World. She thought I missed you, which I can assure you was not the case. Squawk!"

"You didn't miss us even a little?" Cindy joked.

Tango answered with a question, "Squawk! Now, why would I miss a group of predators roaming around my territory?"

Rex nodded, "He has a point."

Tango continued, "Squawk! OK, OK, everything else aside, I kept the pressure on. I told myself she would never feel peace again unless she stopped and truly listened to me. You all know how dense these humans can be sometimes. Squawk!"

"So, what was the turning point? How did you get her to understand?" Rex asked.

"Squawk! Well, I finally did what all good parrots should do in situations like this and started to peck her head. I gave her a few good skull crackers and believe you me she took notice. She threatened to swat me with a newspaper but I flew high and kept up the pressure. Finally, when she was close to losing her mind, she asked point-blank if you animals were trying to get to Mouse World. If I could, I would have laid an egg right then and there. Squawk!"

The human seemed to notice that we were making noises to one another, but had no clue we were maintaining an intelligent conversation. To humans, it sounds like we are chirping or meowing, but , we are conversing. Maybe this human suspected something, but she would never fully understand.

She finally called back to us, "Are you good friends talking back there? What are you saying? Come on, Tango, what are you and friends talking about?"

I turned to Tango and said, "Tell her."

"Squawk! Cats go to Mouse World! Cats go to Mouse World! Squawk!"

I could see in the rear view mirror that the human's eyes were bugging out. "I knew it! I knew you were holding a conversation. Don't any of you little angels worry one bit. I'm going to press down on the gas pedal and get us there in a jiffy. Next stop, Mouse World!"

"Squawk! See, cats... I have her trained. Squawk!"

13

Welcome to Mouse World

We drove all through the night and just as the sun started to climb into the sky, Tango's human announced, "We're here." We all jumped up and stared out the window. What we saw was something that none of us could have comprehended. For a human, it must have been like looking at paradise, but for a cat it was like looking into a nightmare.

We were in a gigantic parking lot that was full of cars and the humans who came from them. Every single light pole had a picture of mouse on it. In fact, there were mice or, more specifically, Marvin pictures everywhere I looked. Every car had a Marvin bumper sticker and the kids all wore Marvin shirts. I even saw some adult humans wearing fake mouse ears.

Cindy spoke first, "Am I dreaming? Please wake me up if I am."

"It's no dream, this is real," Rex replied.

The main park was far away but I could see the giant mouse statues guarding the entranceway. In case you're wondering, it was horrifying.

"Well, we're here. Now what's supposed to happen?" Cindy asked.

I wasn't one hundred percent sure how to answer that question. Somewhere inside of this massive park were a giant mouse and his wife. Somewhere inside of this massive park were my humans. Now, the thing I was purposely not bringing up was the fact that I had no clue as to how we would find any of them and the fact that, for all I knew, there could be a whole family of giant mice living in the park.

Our chauffer seemed to be in shock at the magnitude of the park. "I've never been inside before. I've heard it can be magical."

I had to admit that the parts of the park we could see from the car were pretty amazing. I could see the tops of giant roller coasters and Ferris wheels. I could see realistic imitations of mountains and skyscrapers. I could smell various meats and sweets. I could see how the humans would love this place. It played right into their never ending quest for thrills and satisfaction for their taste buds. Well, who can blame them for thinking of their taste buds?

We all stepped out of the car and mentally prepared ourselves to make the walk into the park. Now, you would think that the sight of a pit bull, three cats, a parrot, and a human all walking together would be a little odd, but not here. Why would it be? Adults of all ages were wearing mouse ears, singing mouse related songs, and generally acting like little kids. Why would a parrot riding on a cat's back make anyone look twice? Yes, I was living in an upside-down world.

We approached one of the many ticketing lines and took our place behind the wave of humanity. Tango's human approached the booth and pulled out her purse. The humans require money for everything and Mouse World was no different.

"Good morning. It will be thirty dollars for a day pass," the young man behind the counter said.

Tango's human pulled out some money and smiled, "That's not so bad. I can't wait to explore the park."

The human handed her a ticket and then spied the rest of us. I thought his eyes would burst from his head. "What in the world is this?"

"Pardon?" Our lady seemed actually surprised that someone would question her little animal parade.

"Ma'am, you can't bring them in here. I mean... I mean... those are dogs and cats."

"Squawk!" Tango interjected.

"Yeah, that's right, there's also a parrot. I can't let you take an entire zoo into Mouse World." The young male dug in his heels. He was going to exercise his authority. In the animal world that's called protecting your territory and is widely accepted as reasonable.

"Oh them, they're harmless. They're my little kiddies," she replied, with a real note of love in her voice.

The ticket taker looked at us for a second and then sheepishly asked, "These are your kids? These are children?"

"Well, of course, they're my little kiddies. I wouldn't have them with me if they weren't," she said giggling.

So for the record, the young man thought we were human children and Tango's human didn't quite grasp what he was asking. To her, kiddies were just an expression of love, but to the young man, we were literally children. Again, humans aren't all that bright.

He looked again and shook his head, "Those outfits are really realistic, especially the parrot. Well, kids are free all day, so I guess you're in the clear. Enjoy your time at Mouse World."

Just like that, we were in the park. The noise level was nearly deafening to my sensitive ears and I can just imagine what the various smells were doing to Tab's delicate nose. Kids were running and screaming at the top of their lungs. They always seemed to have a different kind of treat in their hands or on their clothes. Parents chased their kids and dutifully stood in the long lines to board a particular ride or buy a particular souvenir. It was complete chaos.

I could imagine my human children were probably having fun. I mean, what could I give them back at our home that would rival any of this? If I had money, I would probably be buying up all of the ice cream and hot dogs I could, as well. I found my heart aching for those crazy humans. Sure, the human male had smelly feet and the human female liked to belch when her mate left the room, but they were always good servants to me. The human children could be annoying with their constant bursts of energy, but I always believed they loved me, as they should. Cats aren't supposed to have feelings like this for their servants. What was wrong with me? Was the magic of Mouse World affecting me?

We walked around for what seemed like an hour looking at all of the sites. On occasion, we would spot a human dropping a part of their snack and then we would have a race to see who would get the delicious morsel. Tab won out most of the time, but I was able to get the occasional piece of bun or cone. Tango was even able to find some tasty peanuts and sunflower seeds. Well, tasty to him at any rate, as I found that kind of thing lacking in flavor. Give me some good old fashioned tuna any day.

Rex was a few feet ahead of me when I suddenly saw him stop and stiffen up. I ran up to where he stood and asked him if he was OK.

"No, Carl; no, I'm not OK," he replied tensely.

"Talk to me, Rex, what's the matter?"

"Carl, take a deep breath and then look over there by the roller coaster line."

I turned and looked and my jaw hit the ground. Standing there, larger than life, was none other than Marvin Mouse.

14

Best Friend

"OK, how are we going to play this?" My question was directed towards Rex. I didn't know if we should launch an immediate attack or if we should do some surveillance work first. The rest of our group had walked out of sight, so it might come down to Rex and I having to take down this massive mouse. This would be the perfect time to have Tab's pit bull teeth at work.

Rex took another long, hard look at Marvin and his eyes narrowed like those of any respectable predator. "We take him down right now!"

Before I could say anything, Rex was flying in the air toward the unsuspecting mouse. It would have been a picture perfect landing with claws and teeth slicing through the air, but it didn't happen. No, fate or should I say, a couple of large human hands intervened.

Rex was mere inches from landing on Marvin when two large hands caught him and threw him into a large sack. The heavyset human tied the sack shut and smiled at what appeared to be a coworker. They were dressed in identical coveralls and had labels that read "Pest Control."

The two began to converse as Marvin started to walk in the direction of a large group of children. This whole process had taken under two minutes and I hadn't even moved an inch. It was like events were happening at lightning speed. The two men began to move away and I quickly went in pursuit.

"If it's not the crazy birds thinking Marvin is a rest stop, it's the cats all thinking he's a quick dinner. It's just crazy, Scotty, crazy I tell ya," one of the men said to the other.

"I'm telling ya, Sonny, it gets old. Why the other day I had a call that a possum was on the grounds and chasing after Marvin. The crazy thing probably thought it was his long lost cousin or something," the one called Scotty replied to his friend.

The two moved toward a small shack that must have served as their office space. Before they could close the door behind them, I slipped through and scurried under a nearby chair. I noticed that one of them had put on cotton gloves before putting his hand inside the bag to retrieve Rex. Rex hissed and spit and let out a blood curling scream, but it was to no avail as they put him in a small cage and locked the door.

"Quit your complaining, cat. I'm going to give you some water and a small snack and then I'm going get the nice animal control people to come and get ya," the one called Sonny said.

"He's a feisty one. Kind of reminds me of my oldest son. Boy that one can raise a stink when he gets mad," Scotty replied.

"Like father, like son," Sonny said with a big belly laugh.

Rex looked dejected. He looked like a cat who couldn't believe his misfortune. Only one day earlier, he had escaped from an animal prison and now it looked as though he could be heading toward another one. There was no way I could directly challenge these two large humans and hope to win, nor was there any way I could slip by them and unlock Rex's cage. The shack was simply too small and I risked detection if I so much as flinched a muscle.

"Man, that burger smell is driving me crazy, Sonny," Scotty said as he peered out the window in the direction of the delightful smell.

Sonny nodded and patted his large belly, "Heh heh, yeah, I hear ya, old buddy. My bottomless pit is in need of a double cheeseburger pronto!"

Scotty seemed to be encouraged by the fact that his friend shared his hunger pains. "Man, can't we wait on dealing with the kitty cat? I mean my stomach is aching. Double cheeseburger, fries, large soda... mmmm... I'm drooling here!"

"All right, all right, but if the boss finds this kitty in here and then he finds out we haven't called animal control, we're going to be in deep," Sonny said grimly.

"Ya know old buddy, that's just a risk we're going to have to take," Scotty replied with a laugh. The two rotund men took one last look at Rex before giving in to their hunger and vacating the small shack.

I might only have minutes to act, so I jumped up on the table that held Rex's cage. The lock was simple and I merely swatted the cage open. Rex nonchalantly walked out and began giving himself a shower.

"Am I missing something here?" I was surprised how calmly he was behaving.

"Nope, I knew you would come and get me out of here," Rex said with a smile.

"What do you mean, you knew that I would come and get you out of here?"

"Carl, you're my best friend. I knew you wouldn't leave me locked up. Despite the fact that you could have made a move on Marvin, I knew you would get me out of here," Rex said as he jumped down from the table.

"Well, I appreciate the good words, but I still think you put a lot of faith in me," I replied.

Rex stopped and stared at me, "Carl, if you had been captured by the hamburger twins, do you think I would make every effort to save you?"

"Well, of course, you're that type of cat," I said.

"It's more than that, buddy. We're best friends. You would do anything for me and I would do anything for you. Sure, we might squabble over a table scrap, but that's no big deal. You have now rescued me twice in the last twenty-four hours. If that's not a best friend, I don't know what is," Rex said.

I paused for a moment and nodded, "Thanks, buddy, but it's you who have shown me the way. You came with me on this crazy trip and despite cages, rain, and a lack of food, you've stuck by me. I won't forget that."

Rex smiled and then suddenly his expression changed. I was suddenly terrified, thinking he must have heard Sonny and Scotty returning. I quickly turned and standing in an open closet were, at least, twelve mice and they all looked like Marvin.

15

Marvin's Family

"Rex, get out of here now! We're outnumbered!" I yelled as I nudged Rex towards the front door. Twelve giant mice were too much for us and a hasty retreat was the only logical option.

Rex stared at the closet for an agonizingly long second before he nodded and followed me to the door. Rex jumped towards the knob and used his landing weight to turn it while I simultaneously sunk my claws into the wood and pulled back. With the door now open, we quickly darted back into Mouse World's madness.

As we bounced like deer through the park, we passed Sonny and Scotty. They both had fresh grease stains on their work shirts and the content look of two satisfied eaters. I know this because it's the look I always get after a particularly good meal. Neither noticed us as they were too immersed in their hamburger and French fries dreams.

"Ya know, Sonny, I think next time I'm getting the triple cheeseburger. Yeah, a man like me needs some calories to get through the day," Scotty said as we passed.

After a few minutes, we spotted a shaded area under a tree off the walking path and used it as a place to catch our breath and analyze what we had just witnessed.

"I'm sure I counted twelve, Carl. Twelve gigantic mice and they all looked like Marvin. What is with this place? The water? Radiation? What is going on?" Rex was agitated and quite alarmed.

"Twelve? It doesn't seem possible. I don't see how there can be enough cheese in this town to support such a large mouse population," I said as I tried to reason with myself.

"I might have stayed and fought if we had Tab, but I don't see how we could take on Marvin's whole family," Rex said.

"No, I know what you mean. But Rex, did that whole scenario seem strange to you?" I asked, as I tilted my head to process all of the thoughts racing through my mind.

"Strange? That depends on your definition of strange. I mean, we're in some kind of mouse amusement park and it's full of large mice that walk on two legs and apparently can communicate with the humans. Nothing you say can seem any stranger than what we are living," Rex replied with both sarcasm and sincerity.

"Ok, Ok, just hear me out. I think your points are valid, by the way. These mice are gigantic and that in itself is bizarre, but there are other things that I can't wrap my paws around. How can mice walk on two legs just like the humans and speak the human language?"

Rex nodded, "Yeah, now that you say it, I agree. Plus, the mice we saw in the closet back there didn't seem to even care that we were there. They didn't even move."

"You're right, they didn't even make a move on us. They didn't run or even make a noise. They just stood there with the same goofy looking smile. I'm really confused now. If you think about it, what do we even know about this mouse?" I asked the last question as I scanned the surrounding area. My eyes stopped on a large wooden sign in the middle of the park.

"We need to get to that sign," I told Rex and started slinking my way towards it.

"What's so special about that sign, Carl?"

We approached the sign and I pointed to the large white letters on the top of it. It read: *The History of Marvin Mouse and Mouse World.*

"I think we're about to get some answers," I said as I pushed myself up on my hind legs to read the information on the sign.

It was 1933 when Michael Marvin decided to build his wonderful home for all the children of the world to visit.

It would be a place to experience sights and sounds that would only be limited by our imagination. Michael envisioned a theme park that would be the preferred destination of all the children of the globe. They would come for the thrill of an exciting ride, the taste of that special sweet and, of course, for the chance to visit the one and only Marvin Mouse. Marvin was the childhood friend that Michael always wished he would have had. Marvin Mouse would become that special friend who could bring a smile to the face of every little boy and girl (and plenty of adults as well). Whether through his movies, toys, or a simple picture taken with a visitor, Marvin has brought joy to millions of children worldwide. Marvin's popularity continues to grow, as does the popularity of the park. We have more thrill rides than any theme park in America. The Mouse family now consists of Marvin's wife Mary, brother Mikey, sister Milly, and old grandpa Moldy. More additions to the Marvin Mouse family are expected soon.

Today, Mouse World welcomes millions of visitors yearly.
Marvin thanks you for visiting Mouse World.

"I think I want to faint. This says there are siblings and even a grandfather. It says there will be more additions soon. What is going on?" Rex asked.

"I don't know and I don't think I want to know. Still, there is something that is bothering me," I told Rex.

"What's that?"

"Michael Marvin? I don't understand why they mention the word *imagination* or why they even talk about this human who created the park," I answered.

Rex nodded, "I see what you mean. Something doesn't add up. So what do you suggest?"

I didn't want to say it, but I didn't think we had a choice, "We need to go back to Sonny and Scotty's shack. We need to confront Marvin's family."

16

Land of Giants

It was amazing that in this theme park, most of the visitors didn't even notice that there were cats running around loose. The humans were so easily hypnotized by the rides, food, and sights of the park. Because of this, we were almost invisible. The humans' turning their attention elsewhere was precisely what I didn't want to happen inside my own home. If it meant taking down twelve gigantic mice to make the world right, then so be it.

We knew that the humans tried at all cost to get through the day and stay as far from work as possible after hours, so we knew it would only be a matter of time before Sonny and Scotty departed for the day. We found a little bush nearby that would camouflage us and then we settled in. We were cats and could sit like statues for hours if necessary. The humans could never outlast us.

It wasn't too long before Sonny and Scott emerged from the shack. By their conversation, it seemed as if they were leaving for the day.

"I don't know what I'm going to do; I might go grab a pizza. Then again, I might go home and grill up a steak. What about you, Sonny?"

"Scotty my boy, I'm going to the rib house. All you can eat ribs for a ten spot. Are you up for a little eating challenge?"

"Now you're speaking my language," Scotty said, laughing.

I have to admit that these two humans weren't so bad. They did have cat like appetites. How could I not respect them?

"So, uh… Scotty…what about that cat that escaped? Do you think anyone will ask about it?" Sonny asked.

"The only person that might even know is ol' Marvin and he isn't going to say anything. He probably already forgot. Look, I don't know how the crazy cat escaped, but it did and that's that. Give the thing some credit, he must have been pretty smart," Sonny replied with a chuckle. With that, the two walked off on their quest to fill their large stomachs with some tasty ribs. There are times I wish I had two legs and some money.

"How are we going to get in? Do you think we could pull off the door opening trick again?" I asked Rex.

Rex nodded and leaped up toward the door knob, while I pushed instead of pulled. In a matter of seconds the door was open and we were standing inside. The closet door was cracked open and we could only assume that Marvin's minions were still inside.

"After you, Rex," I said as I smiled.

"No, after you, old buddy," Rex returned.

"Yeah, I guess it's my fault we're even here, so I should be the first one to be made into a cat sandwich," I mumbled. I used my body to open the door further and took my first steps inside of the closet.

I found myself standing a few inches from a giant mouse foot. My eyes adjusted to the dimly lit closet and I noticed there were mice feet everywhere. A chill went down my spine as I whispered for Rex to enter. For whatever reason, the mice were not running, attacking, or even making any noise. I had watched enough of the human Japanese monster movies to know that in most cases, giant mutant lizards and moths like to move and destroy and they are never the quiet types. These mice were as quiet as church mi… well, you get the point. Something was wrong.

Rex and I looked at each other and communicated with our eyes. I would try the diplomatic approach and see if I could talk them into leaving Mouse World immediately and to promise to stop brainwashing our humans.

I cleared my throat and began, "Excuse me, can I have your attention? My name is Carl and I am here with a cat, dog, and parrot contingent. We are here to ask-no, demand-that you and your leader, Marvin Mouse vacate Mouse World and return to whatever island, galaxy, or bad dream you came from."

Rex shook his head, "Maybe a little strong, Carl."

I nodded and waited for a mouse reply, but no sound came. Did these mice not speak the universal animal language? Had all their years with humans made it so they only spoke the human tongue? No, that can't be it. They should have said something at the mere sight of us.

I decided to try an intimidation tactic. I hissed and spit. I took the scary cat approach and made a high arch with my back. I showed my fangs and even let out a blood curling screech. The mice stayed frozen.

"Something is wrong. You scared me with that, but they didn't do a thing," Rex said, shaking his head.

"I don't get it. They just keep staring straight ahead. Well, I guess we only have option left and that is to attack!" I was already airborne as I screamed out the last word. Rex followed my lead.

We slammed into the chest of the first mouse which resulted in the mouse, Rex, and me crashing to the floor. Again there was no noise from the mice or turmoil from the others. In fact, I noticed that the mouse I had attacked was completely flat.

"It's not real," an astonished Rex said.

"No, it's not. It's just a mouse costume!" I cried out.

"We looked around and saw that all of the mice were just costumes that were attached to hooks. In fact, we found folded up Marvin and Mary outfits in a box at the rear of the closet. I wasn't entirely sure what this meant. Did this mean Marvin and Mary were elaborate frauds? Were they fakes designed to trick the humans out of their money? Were they put here to interfere with cat dominance in the world? Were Marvin and Mary real and these outfits just another way for the humans to honor them by dressing up as them?

"Stupid cats."

"Did you just say, "Stupid cats'?" Rex asked me.

"No, I thought it was you. At least, I was hoping it was you," I told him with the sudden awareness that we were being watched.

"Up here, dumb dumbs."

We looked up and sitting in a small cage on the shelf was something small and white. It was a mouse. Rex and I jumped up to the shelf and eyed the small creature.

"Allow me to introduce myself, my name is Marvin Mouse."

17

Marvin

"You're Marvin Mouse?" Rex asked. We both tried to stifle our laughter.

"The one and only, my mindless felines," the little mouse quickly answered back.

I studied him intently and shook my head. "No, it's impossible. Humans count the days differently from animals, but there is no way you're the inspiration for Mouse World. It doesn't add up. You're only a few years old at most."

"No kidding, you're a regular Sherlock Holmes," the little mouse answered sarcastically.

"So, you agree that you're not Marvin Mouse?" Rex asked.

"Do you agree that you're goofy? I said my name is Marvin Mouse and I am indeed Marvin Mouse," he answered.

Cats are curious by nature and Rex and I could keep these questions going for hours, but the time for delay was long since past. I was not going to have this little smart mouth mouse continue to keep us in the dark.

"Look, you rat wannabe, you're going to stop the nonsense and tell us how it is that you're Marvin Mouse!" I yelled and hissed.

"What if I refuse, whisker boy?" the little mouse fired back. My patience was really being tested with this one.

"If you refuse, my friend and I are going swat this cage to the floor, break it open, and have ourselves a tasty mouse sandwich!" I threatened.

The little mouse paced back in forth for a few minutes, seemingly lost in thought. Finally, he shrugged his little shoulders and said, "OK, OK, you win. It's just that I don't have many opportunities to play cat and mouse."

"Well, all is forgiven if you'll just answer our questions," Rex said.

The mouse didn't seem scared necessarily, but he wasn't going to play around anymore with the dangling prospect that he could wind up a tasty snack. "Well, I'm sure you two dopes... I mean, cats... know about Michael Marvin. He's the human who started this whole mouse park."

"We know all about him, you just need to tell us how you can be Marvin Mouse," I pressed.

"Chill out, fish breath, I'm getting there. You see, Michael was a lonely kid and didn't have many kids his age living around him, so he decided to create a friend," the little mouse said.

"So, are we to assume you're that friend?" Rex interrupted.

"Would you mind keeping your mouth zipped while I tell the story? If you two litter lovers keep it up, we'll be here all day," the mouse said in a tone that expressed frustration.

"Sure, we'll shut it. Just get on with it," I told him.

The mouse looked up as he thought and then continued, "You see, Michael needed a friend just like we all do, so he invented one. He made an imaginary friend. I guess he decided that an imaginary human friend would be boring, so he came up with a mouse friend. No offense, but he picked the superior animal."

Rex and I looked at one another, but didn't comment.

Marvin continued, "Michael's parents grew concerned and decided that it would be OK to give the little guy a breathing friend and so they gave him a little mouse. Michael loved it and named it Marvin. Before too long, he had saved up some allowance and bought a Mary. One thing led to another and he had this huge family of mice. You see, that original pair of mice is my great-great-great grandfather and grandmother. I'm not the original, but I can assure you I am Marvin Mouse."

"Well, this changes everything... well, at least I think it does..." Rex said as he looked at me.

"I don't get it. Why the giant mouse costumes? Why the deception?" I needed some answers before I decided the next move.

The mouse didn't seem bothered by my questions and he dutifully answered. "Yeah, there is a deception of sorts, but there is a reason for it. You see, for right or wrong-and I think it's wrong-there are a lot of humans who don't like little squeaky mice."

"Well, who can blame them?" Rex asked with a smile. I nodded in agreement.

The mouse quickly fired back, "Yeah, and who can blame all the poor little doggies who like to chew up cats? You see, Michael grew up to be a smart businessman and he recognized that there were probably a lot of other kids out there who needed friends or at least needed a friendly and reliable playmate whenever they wanted. He also knew that as you grew up, the need for friends and family doesn't go away, but in fact grows even stronger."

"Yeah, I can see that..." I said as I looked at Rex and thought of Mars and Cindy. I thought of my own family and how much I needed and relied on their love.

The mouse continued, "Michael decided to create a place for people of all ages to come and visit. It would be a place of great wonder and a place where anything was possible. This is why you have rides where you see friendly monsters and talking animals. This was all created so families could come and spend time together and just escape the realities of everyday life."

Rex nodded and asked, "How did it come to be known as Mouse World then?"

"Well, he knew that a park like this needed a spokesperson. It needed someone to be the unofficial leader of all the crazy creatures that lived here. He wanted it to be a way to honor his friend and inspiration. He wanted it to honor the original Marvin Mouse. He knew that people would never go for a mouse the way God made them, but they would go for a cartoony mouse that spoke like the humans and even kind of resembled them in that he wore clothes and how he walked on two legs. Michael was a man with a vision, but I don't think he ever knew that Marvin would be so universally loved," the young mouse said.

"I hate to admit it, but my humans love him more than they love me," I answered with sadness. There wasn't a giant mouse after all. This was yet another creation by the humans. Yes, it did honor mice, but it only honored an imaginary mouse. How do I fight that?

18

An Unlikely Alliance

The mouse shook his head and eyed me. "Are you done feeling sorry for yourself, Mr. Cat? Do you need me to get you one of the human handkerchiefs so you can wipe your little yellow eyes?"

"Hey, lay off him!" Rex hissed.

I calmly looked at the mouse and said, "No, I don't need a handkerchief. I've spoken the truth and, I guess, I just have to live with it. My humans have chosen this mouse fantasy land over me. I had thought I could come down here and maybe run this giant mouse off, but now I find out the whole thing is an illusion. It is what it is. Why pretend it's not?"

"Wow, cats really are wimps. Look at you. You have size, warm fur, and a little bit of freedom. Me? I'm stuck in a cage, most women are scared of me, and every cat, dog, bird, and snake wants to eat me for lunch. I guess

I'm the crazy one. I should be happy. I mean, after all, look at how bad the poor cat has it," Marvin said with words just dripping in sarcasm.

"You need to leave him alone or I'll have you for lunch!" Rex yelled out in my defense.

"Nah, leave him alone, Rex. He's right. I am holding a little pity party. I've done it once before and you set me straight. I have a lot going for me and I have something else that all cats have and that's a sense of optimism."

Rex looked puzzled, "What do you mean?"

I looked at Marvin and smiled, "I've learned on this trip to never dismiss the idea of new friends. Sometimes you have to put aside the stereotypes and give someone new a chance in your life. Marvin, I want to offer you my friendship and, if you'll take it, I want to form a pact."

Rex scratched himself, "Whoa, Carl, are you talking about a mouse and cat alliance?"

"None other. I've become friends with a pit bull and a parrot, so why not a mouse? I can either sit around feeling sorry for myself or I can create some happy things in my life," I said.

"What's your name, by the way?" Marvin asked.

"My name is Carl and my friend here is Rex."

The mouse tilted his head in the universal animal processing sign. "Friends spend time together. What kind of things do you have in mind for us?"

"Well for starters, I want us to go find my other friends. I want to tell them that I was wrong. I was wrong about this whole thing. There is no giant family of mutant mice and instead of chasing any mice out of town, I'm going to make friends with one. I also want to try to find my humans and to let them know that I love them and that my love is unconditional. If they want to love an imaginary giant mouse, then it's OK. I can live with it. I have made some new friendships and reinforced some old ones. I'm blessed and I want the world to know it."

Rex looked at me with admiration, "That was incredible, Carl. I think I need to start appreciating my surroundings more. My humans aren't perfect, but I didn't get this stomach from eating rocks and dirt. They've always fed me pretty well."

The mouse laughed, "From the looks of that stomach, I think you've been eating nothing but straight bacon."

"Watch it, mouse," Rex replied.

Marvin turned to me and said, "Well Carl, I can appreciate your words, but I also want to come with you. For the most part, I'm just a prop here. Michael is an old man now and it seems like his family keeps me tucked away in here all the time. They haul me out to show their friends whenever they want to tell the story about the real Marvin Mouse, but otherwise, I'm lonely. I want to find

Michael and tell him goodbye and then maybe find a nice mouse hole to raise a family in. Would you take me to Michael?"

"You point the way and I promise I'll do that very thing," I answered.

Marvin paced back and forth mumbling to himself. He was obviously tempted, but for a mouse to become friends with a cat was a serious leap of faith. I mean, what if there was a sudden shortage on cat food? What if one of my cat friends lost control? For Marvin, it was a far riskier proposition than for me.

"Well, Mr. Cat... I would be honored to be your friend."

Rex laughed and shook his head in amazement, "I never thought I would witness this day."

I had peace in my heart and that peace felt good. The old wars were over and the days of self-pity were gone as well. We would never be as things were in Egypt and that was OK. I had always looked around and blamed circumstances instead of just admitting my faults and making an effort to improve. I had crossed the bridge and now had a chance at a new and improved life. I needed to find Michael, my humans, and of course, my friends. After that, I needed to go home.

"Rex, old buddy?"

"Yeah, Carl."

"Let's spring Marvin from his cell and get outside. We have a cat, dog, parrot, and a bunch of humans to find."

19

Goodbye Michael

It was the middle of the night and we prowled the amusement park without any problems. We would merely jump in a bush or hide behind a trash can whenever we smelled a security guard and we were always far to fast for any of the various cleaning machines buffing up the park in anticipation of the next day.

Marvin had remarkable instinct and expertly guided us to the large mansion in the center of the park. We stopped at the long walkway and peered up to the top of the mansion where we could see a light was turned on.

"What is this place?" Rex asked.

Marvin looked up and smiled, "This is Michael's home. In a way, this is my home. I was born here."

"Michael actually lives here?" I asked.

"Yes. He has for years. He always wanted to be close to the action. My father told me that when Michael was younger, he would venture out into the park to shake hands, share rides, and to see the smiles on the faces of all the children," Marvin said. I could tell that his mind was taking him back to what was probably a better time.

"Does he ever leave his home?" Rex asked.

"Not like in the old days. He's much older and he's slowed down. I think he's forgotten a lot of things and that includes me. I still feel like I owe him a goodbye. Without him or his vision, I wouldn't be standing here," Marvin answered.

"Well, as much as I love the view, we need to get up there and give you some time with Michael. Plus, I have to admit, I want to see the man who started all of this," I said.

The three of us proceeded down the walkway and entered the grand mansion through a motion sensor door. There was an empty work station where a secretary probably sat during the daytime, but other than that, the path to the elevator was clear. Rex put the mouse on his head and then stood up on his hind legs. This allowed Marvin to hit the button that would send the elevator to Michael's quarters.

The elevator moved quickly, but the ride was quiet. The little mouse seemed depressed, since he was going into this with the attitude that he would soon be saying goodbye to his old life. More often than not, it is the human who says goodbye to the animal and not the other way around. The humans may have been given inferior looks, smell, and intelligence compared to us, but they were blessed with a longer life. Who said life was fair?

The elevator stopped and opened up into Michael's private suite. It occurred to me that security was really lax, but I just figured that Michael had the kind of life that had no secrets. He was as much a part of his park as Marvin Mouse.

The room was well lit and full of fine furniture. It seemed like it was lived in, but it also seemed strangely cold and distant. Rex found drawings of mice on one desk and there was an open book on the nightstand in the bedroom. We checked every single room, but there was no sign of Michael Marvin.

"When was the last time you actually saw Michael?" I asked.

"Not since I was a baby, to be honest. My memory is programmed for remembering cheese, so I could be mistaken about that, though. The humans always just hauled me out for their friends to see and said I was Michael's mouse. I don't recall him being at any of those meetings now that I think about it," Marvin answered.

Rex shrugged his shoulders, "What do you think Carl? He's obviously not here and to tell you the truth, everything looks kind of off."

"There's always one way to tell if he actually lives here and that is by checking the refrigerator. Eating large amounts of food is what animals and humans have in common," I said as I sprang toward the kitchen.

The refrigerator was propped open and inside were what looked like a glass of milk, a plate of cookies, and a small block of cheddar cheese. Like everything else in the living space, something didn't seem quite right. It didn't give off a smell and it had a plastic like look to it. As I was processing the situation, Marvin leapt off of Rex and toward the cheese. He ran up and took a bite but recoiled at the taste.

"Yuck! It's not real!" the little mouse yelled out in horror.

Rex sniffed the milk and cookies and confirmed that they, too, were nothing but fakes. The humans could often be mysterious, but this was taking things to a new level.

"Carl, there's a note on the kitchen table. Let's take a look." Rex said as he leaped on the table. He grabbed it in his mouth and rejoined us on the floor.

"One of you guys read it, my human is a little rusty," Marvin said.

Michael Marvin's Kitchen

Mr. Marvin's kitchen is the same as it has been since his passing. The refrigerator holds copies of the treats that Michael and Marvin enjoyed when spending time together. Michael would often sit at this very table eating cookies and drinking a cold glass of milk and right beside him sat his trusted friend Marvin, enjoying some fresh cheese.

"What does 'passing' mean?" Marvin asked.

Rex looked at me and nodded his head. I agreed that there was no sense hiding it from the little guy. "I think it means that Michael is in heaven now." Marvin's eyes grew wide.

"I'm sorry, Marvin," Rex said glumly.

"Wow, he's gone …" Marvin's voice trailed.

"He was happy when he left," someone said from under the refrigerator. An elderly mouse emerged and moved towards us. He wasn't the least bit alarmed by us. I quickly noticed that there was something familiar about this mouse. Marvin quickly noticed it as well.

"Dad?"

The elderly mouse touched noses with Marvin and laughed, "It is you. Son, I thought I would never see you again. Once I was retired, I heard rumblings that future Marvin's would only be used for corporate functions. I just figured you had found a home at some bigwig's house and left the park for good."

"Well, I found a home all right, but it was in a closet down in the pest control shack with two men with appetites that would make a hyena blush," Marvin answered with some of his wise cracking reemerging.

"Well, the elephants in the room are these two felines, so I had better ask: why in the world is my son running around with two cats?" The old mouse eyed us suspiciously.

20

Reunion

It was quite the sight. It's not every day that cats and mice sit around and discuss the various happenings in their lives. I could just imagine Tab or Cindy walking in and seeing this scene. Pausing to rest and reflect was not only the right thing to do since Marvin and his father were now reunited, but it cleared up some more of the mystery surrounding Michael and it allowed us to re-energize before the park opened again, at which time I could find my friends and my humans.

Marvin's father had been living a life of semi-seclusion the last few years. He told us that around the time when Michael's health started to fail, he had been granted his freedom. Michael's family members saw that the senior Marvin was slowing down and thought that by putting his son in the limelight, it might reignite the sparkle in old Michael's eyes. Michael, like all of us will be, was physically tired and started to retreat from his day to day activities. This included his interaction with his beloved mouse. Michael's memory faded with his health and before long, Marvin was just another pet to be kept in a cage and brought out when it was time for a good story.

Marvin's father was released into the wild just outside the park. Now, keep in mind that this is Texas which means there are a lot of hungry snakes and other creatures of the night prowling around. Well, I guess I have to be fair: there are also a lot of young cats prowling around. For a mouse, especially an elderly mouse that has always lived like a human, it was quite the experience.

Marvin's father told us stories about evading every kind of predator and mouse trap imaginable before finally spotting the only home he had ever known, Mouse World. He managed to avoid Sonny and Scotty and make his way back to the castle. It took him close to a year before he could make his way back to Michael's room and establish himself a nice den in one of the cupboards. He had arrived too late to see his son removed, but he was there at the end for his old master.

"He was a good friend to me. I miss him dearly," the elderly mouse told his son.

"I never really had a chance to get to know him. My time with him was short," Marvin said sadly.

"Now, don't you be getting sad on me. Michael lived a good life. In fact, he lived the life he wanted to live. He had a lot of friends and he made a lot of people happy. You, me, and our ancestors were and are a part of that. The Marvin Mouse that greets people here may be a human in a silly costume, but he's a part of us. He wouldn't even be there if it hadn't been for mice like us and a creative mind like Michael's. I miss him every day, but I'm thankful I even had the chance to know him," the elder mouse said.

"I guess you're right, but…," Marvin's voice trailed off.

Marvin's father stared at him long and hard anticipating the "but" Marvin had spoken.

"Dad, I don't want you to be upset, but I think I'm going to be leaving Mouse World. The humans seem to have things under control and I'm confident our legacy is intact," Marvin told his father. Marvin felt he needed to get right to the point and he didn't fail.

The elder mouse thought long and hard and then he turned to study Rex and me. I had never known mice to be so intelligent. It was yet another one of the stereotypes I had built up, now being broken down. It was like a weight had been lifted off my shoulder. I just didn't want to carry the weight of distrust and dislike any longer.

"You sure have been looking at us a long time," Rex said to the elder Marvin.

"Yeah, Dad, what's the matter?" The younger Marvin seemed to be getting uncomfortable.

"I just can't believe my own flesh and blood would be hanging around a couple of cats. No offense, but this is crazy." The older mouse still seemed in shock that we were friendly with his son.

"He must have taste," Rex replied.

"Yeah, but you better not ever get a taste for him!" The elder mouse said threateningly.

I had to laugh, even though that was risking angering the elder Marvin. "We give our word; he'll be safe with us. My mouse-chasing days are over. I just want to find my friends and my humans and get back home."

"I agree, it's time to get home," Rex nodded.

"They're good cats and we made a promise to each other. You trusted a human and it's not like mice and humans have a picture perfect relationship. It's time to extend some trust to these guys as well," the little mouse said seeming to take on the role of a diplomat with his words.

The elder mouse continued to study us and then slowly nodded his head, "Yeah, maybe it is time to put the old grudges aside. Maybe it'll add some years to my life." He laughed and turned back to his son. "Now what do you mean you want to leave Mouse World? Weren't you listening to my story? There are some serious obstacles awaiting you outside that park."

The younger mouse looked at us and then back at his father. He seemed to grow in strength. "Dad, it's time I go. You're my father and I'll always love you. Mouse World will always have a place in my heart, but I need to go. I need to be free. I hope you can understand."

The older mouse nodded with acceptance and rubbed noses with his son. "Marvin, you're just like Michael. You're a brave dreamer. I think Michael would have been proud of you. I know that I'm very proud of you."

I almost had a tear in my eye as I witnessed the touching scene. Cats don't usually form relationships with their fathers and suddenly I was regretting that. Marvin didn't get the chance to say goodbye to Michael personally, but in a way, he said goodbye through his father. He also had the peace and comfort of knowing he could go out in the world with his father's blessing and love.

21

Friends United

The park was already jam packed with humans when we decided to begin our search for Tab, Cindy, and Tango. We knew they were probably worried that we were still missing and that they were desperate to find us. Rex let Marvin ride on his back as we moved between trash cans and concession booths looking for our friends.

Marvin enjoyed getting a lift from Rex and made sure to tell him, "Ride' em, cow-mouse!"

"It was somewhat amusing the first time you said it, but if I were you, I wouldn't push my luck," Rex said, only half joking. It's one thing to be friends with a cat, but one should never push their luck by making fun of one. We were still wild animals after all.

We had discussed it and figured that the best area to find Tab or Cindy would be near one of the hamburger stands. Dogs have notorious appetites for beef and Cindy just had a notorious appetite period. It would only be a matter of time before one of those two was pulled to the hamburger stand like a paper clip to a large magnet.

I have to admit that my stomach was growling pretty hard, but I knew if we could find Tango's human, she would make sure we were filled back up. The little mouse crumbs that Marvin's father served us were nice, but they could hardly satisfy Rex and me.

"Well, how long do you think it will take before they come?" Rex asked.

"Hmmm… it's almost lunch time, so I'm guessing Cindy's second breakfast is about wearing off. I would say that we will either see them in a few minutes or we'll hear some serious begging," I replied to my friend.

We were enjoying a nice laugh when panic started to grip me. Cats have a sixth sense in this regard. I couldn't figure out why I was getting so worried. I looked around and then I smelled the air. I smelled something familiar, but I couldn't figure out what it was.

"What's the matter?" Marvin asked, once he noticed my pacing.

"I'm not sure yet..." I said with my voice trailing off.

"You're right Carl, something is wrong," Rex said. Rex's confirmation of the situation made me even more confident that something unsettling was about to happen. As soon as my thought had ended, the reason or should I say, reasons-for my fear appeared.

"There they are!" It was Scotty yelling and pointing in our direction. Sonny smiled and began moving in our direction. How could I be so dumb? These two humans had appetites that rivaled any animal and so naturally they would be drawn to the tempting smells of cooked hamburger.

Sonny bent over and tried to coax me to him, "Here kitty, kitty, kitty. Come to nice Sonny, little kitty." If this goof thought I was going to fall for "here kitty, kitty," he had another thing coming.

"What should we do?" Marvin cried out.

"Run!" I yelled. We leaped away from the approaching hands of our would-be captors and moved with lighting speed into the lines of people awaiting their turn to order a delicious snack.

"Sonny, move it, we need to catch them!" Scotty yelled out. He was the faster of the two and quickly started in hot pursuit.

"Scotty, I think that orange cat has Marvin with them. We have to save Marvin!" It must have puzzled Sonny that Marvin was riding on the back of a cat, but I didn't hear him mention that part. Whether these two were worried that they would be fired for losing Marvin or they envisioned great riches from bringing him home is hard to

178

say, but what I could say is that they had no intention of giving up the chase.

Rex pulled next to me and said, "Carl, we can both go high into the trees and risk a firefighter coming to snatch us or a bird trying to grab Marvin, or we can put our heads down and hit the burners. Either way, we need to make a decision soon. I'm tired and hungry and quickly losing my energy."

"The trees won't work. We would be trapped. Let's go full speed ahead. If worse comes to worst, and one of us is near capture, the other one needs to make a hard turn and try to find somewhere safe to hide until nightfall." I didn't want to split up and yet, there was no sense in us both being caught. For two large, hamburger eating men, these two weren't giving up. I guess hamburgers can give you a lot of energy.

People were stopping and staring at the strange sight of two overgrown men chasing two cats and a mouse through the park. Pictures were being taken and, occasionally, a round of applause would break out. My legs were burning and my mouth was dry. My years of couch lounging were catching up to me. Rex was an outside cat and a whole lot stronger than me, so he had a real chance of escape. I needed to do the right thing here. Sacrificing for my friend was really no sacrifice at all, so I began to slow down and prepare for capture.

"Gotcha!" Sonny yelled out as he grabbed me and pulled me close. I was too weak to scratch or bite. I fell into his fried grease smelling t-shirt and hoped Rex could get away.

Scotty stopped and tried to catch his breath, "You did it, Sonny. You caught one of them."

"Yeah, I caught one of them, but you're letting Marvin and the other cat get away. Get moving, you goof!" Sonny yelled out.

I could see from the corner of my eye that Scotty wasn't moving. Scotty turned to Sonny with a look of fear in his eye. "Uh… Sonny?"

Sonny was still admiring his capture, but he answered, "What is it? Why aren't you trying to get Marvin?"

"Sonny… uh… would you mind looking…" Scotty's voice trailed off. Sonny turned to look and his mouth fell open.

"That's a pit bull… a very angry pit bull…" Sonny mumbled.

Tab stood there curling his lip and baring his teeth. He growled so hard that it seemed like it would have been impossible for him to even take a breath. Scotty and Sonny were both shaking. I took advantage of Scotty's frozen state to jump to the ground and make my way to where my friend was standing.

"Hello, Tab," I said with relief.

"Once again, the dog has to come to the rescue," he replied through clenched teeth.

"G-g-g-good puppy," Sonny said. Both men started to slink backward as they, undoubtedly, hoped that Tab wouldn't begin a pursuit.

Tango flew up and landed on Tab's back and gave the order, "Sic 'em, Tab!"

Tab leaped after the now running Sonny and Scotty and chased them a few dozen yards before stopping and returning to where we stood. I was so happy to see him and, for that matter, all of my friends. Rex and Marvin received lots of pets from Tango's human and Cindy was crying out with meows of joy. It's always nice to know that you are loved.

"It's good to see all of you, it's really good," I said. The excitement of the chase was still buzzing through my body, but it was quickly replaced by the comfort of friends.

The large crowd that had gathered around us for the climax of the show had dispersed. None of them were even aware that nothing was staged and we were all real animals. I had overheard one boy say he wanted a costume like the pit bull.

Rex came over to me and said, "You took one for the team, Carl. You put yourself before Marvin and me. Thank you, old buddy."

"You're welcome, Rex. You would have done the same for me."

Tango's human inspected both of us and shook her head with concern, "You poor things look famished. I don't know where you've been or why those mean young men were chasing you, but I do know that you need a good meal. I'll be right back. I think I saw a fish stand around the corner." Yes, she was a good human.

Rex turned to Cindy, "Well, did you miss us, Cindy?"

Cindy didn't miss a beat, "Hmm... let's see... I went on some fun rides with Tab and Tango. Tango's human fed us all kinds of tasty snacks. We stayed in a nice hotel room near the park and stayed up late watching television and snacking some more. I had a nice breakfast and a quick cat nap. So, did I miss you? Hmm... I think I'll pass on that answer."

"I was just thinking that it's good to be loved," I laughed.

Rex shook his head, "We've been gone for a whole night? Wow..."

"Squawk! Where have you two liver-eaters been? Squawk!" Tango was his usual self and I loved every last "squawk".

"It's not important, what's important is that we found each other. I've decided that this trip was made for the wrong reasons, but I'm thankful that it allowed me to meet some new friends," I said.

"Squawk! Speaking of which, what's with the little rat? Squawk!" Tango asked.

Marvin looked shocked at the statement and returned fire accordingly, "I'm actually Marvin Mouse. What's your name, Mr. Parakeet?"

"Squawk! Touché. Squawk!"

"Did you say Marvin Mouse?" Tab asked.

"The one and only. I'm pleased to meet all of you," Marvin said with confidence.

"I'm not following…" Cindy's voice trailed off as she tried to process how a little mouse could be the Marvin that we had set out to find.

Rex jumped in, "Well, you see, we actually found a closet full of giant Marvin's but they weren't really Marvin's. You see, they were actually costumes, well, costumes for humans. You see, Marvin is this little guy: well, he's one of the Marvin's. He's actually the descendant of the original Marvin, which was actually the brainchild of Michael Marvin and was… I need to stop, I'm getting dizzy."

Tab's eyes grew wide and he smelled Marvin, "So, we came all the way down here to confront a giant mouse and instead it's just this little guy? I'm not sure if I should be glad or angry."

"Please be glad…" Rex told Tab only half-jokingly.

"I'm still confused," Cindy said with a cocked head.

"It doesn't really matter. What matters is that this is a place for humans to come and have fun. It was a mistake to come here with any bad intentions. However, I'm thankful that I did. Marvin is my friend and I'm grateful for that," I said to the approving nods of my friends.

"You aren't so bad yourself my hairball coughing pal," the little mouse said, laughing.

"Squawk! Hairball? Ha ha…I like this little guy! Squawk!" Tango couldn't resist.

"We like him as well and we promised him that he would be safe with us," Rex added.

"Are you listening, Cindy?" I asked.

Cindy was studying Marvin and licking her lips, but quickly snapped out of it, "Sorry, old habits die hard." We all shared a laugh.

Tango's human returned with fish sticks and hamburgers and we all enjoyed a nice lunch on one of the picnic benches. It felt good to have a full stomach again and I decided to treat myself to a quick shower before departing to find my humans. If they were still at the park, I would find them.

22

Family Reunited

"So where should we look first?" Rex asked. I was leading the group into the park on a quest to find my humans. I missed the little girls and wanted to feel their petting and hear their praise. I missed the human female filling my food bowl so faithfully every morning. I even missed the human male yelling at me for sharpening my claws on his favorite chair. It felt good to be reunited with my friends, but I needed my family. I had been arrogant and dismissive of them for too long. If I would be allowed to have one more chance with them, I would make things right. Fortunately for me, that chance was literally around the corner.

I didn't know how it all came together at the time, but Tango later told me how his human had a rather interesting encounter while waiting in line to buy us some much needed fish sticks. She was patiently waiting in the long line when she overheard a female voice saying, "Look girls, think what Carl would do if he could taste some of that fish."

Tango's human turned to smile at the family unit of a father, mother, and two girls. She asked, "Is Carl your cat?"

The oldest girl laughed, "My daddy says Carl is a pig, but yeah, I guess he's a cat."

The human father gently shook his head, "Yes, ma'am, we have a cat back home with a big appetite. My wife was just commenting on how he would go crazy if he ever tasted the fish they are serving."

Tango's human bent over and kindly spoke to the two little girls, "If you two girls like cats, you should come and see who is with me. I have three cats, one dog, one parrot, and even a little mouse."

The girls smiled and looked at her suspiciously and then up at their parents. The human mother nodded her head and said, "Well, if she says she has them, then she must have them."

The older of the two girls asked, "Can we go Mommy, can we go?"

The younger girl echoed her sister and pleaded, "Please Mommy. Can we see the animals?" It turns out that my humans had been thinking of me all along.

The human mother looked at her husband and he nodded. Tango's human led them to us. The whole family was soon making its way through the crowd and toward our group. The first voice I heard was that of the human father. "That orange cat looks like the one that always meows outside our windows and that chubby female looks like the cat who always chases our birds away."

"Squawk! That's ridiculous! Squawk!" Tango yelled out.

The human male was my human servant... err... I mean human alpha male. I couldn't believe it was him. I knew they were here, of course, but there was a part of me starting to doubt I would ever see them again. He hadn't noticed me yet, nor had the human female who was looking with amazement at the talking parrot. The two little girls Hailey, and Sydney, saw me first. Yes, they have names. Usually, we cats don't pay attention to our servants... err... I mean human partners names, but now I needed to do so. I loved them and I needed to respect them. They were my girls.

Hailey's eyes grew wide, "Mommy, that's Carl!"

The mother, Nina, squinted and said in a flurry, "No, that can't be. I just spoke to Aunt Patricia this morning and she said Carl was doing just fine back home. There's no way a cat could make it all the way to Mouse World. But I have to admit... it sure does look like Carl."

The father, Nicholas was also squinting, "That really does look like Carl. Wow, that's uncanny."

The girls were petting and hugging me and I was soaking it all in. Nicholas was still skeptical and turned to Tango's human, Margaret, and said, "Ma'am, where did you get that cat?"

"I just found him. Actually, with the exception of my beautiful Tango, I found all of them. Well, all of them but the mouse, I'm not sure where he came from," Margaret answered.

"Nick, he acts like he knows us," Nina was in shock and I can't say I blame her. She started petting me and I rubbed up against her like I do when I want my breakfast.

"But, Aunt Patricia... you said that she said that Carl was with her and he was getting along with Bella. I mean, this can't be our Carl," Nick responded. He was trying to convince himself that the impossible hadn't just happened.

Hailey and Sydney knew the truth and they turned to their mother. Hailey spoke and Sydney nodded,

"Mommy, it's him. I know it in my heart. It's our Carl."
Nina smiled and then I knew. She knew it in her heart as well.

Nina turned to Nick, "It's him, Nick. I don't know how it's possible, but it's him."

Nick shook his head in amazement, "Then who does Aunt Patricia have? Does Carl have a twin we don't know about?"

Sydney spoke up, "Daddy, it must be that crazy brown tabby we saw fall out of the tree that one day."

Nick nodded, "Yeah, that's that Marsik or Mars. I remember him getting stuck in the street drain one time. Yeah, I guess he could pass for our Carl."

I didn't know Mars had such a reputation, but no matter. I was reunited with my family and that's all that mattered.

Margaret was able to get everyone's attention when she said, "Now, I don't speak cat, of course, but if you ask me, I think this little Carl and his friends either wanted to come down here to catch that Marvin Mouse or they wanted to see you. They can be driven creatures, you know."

My family was studying me and, undoubtedly, their brains were turning. How could a cat and a group of animals find their humans in an amusement park so far away from home? I was starting to think that I might have made a mistake. My family might decide to send me to one of those pet shows they were always watching. I might end up as one of those animals who have to go on television and do some crazy stunt to the amusement of the humans.

"They certainly are," Nina trailed off. She looked at the girls and then back to her husband. I could tell she wanted to ask him something. I had witnessed this being played out many times before.

Nick looked at Nina and started to shake his head, "No, no, absolutely not, Nina. If you're getting ready to ask me to bring this… this… zoo back home with us, you're crazy."

Nina implored, "Please, Nick, we can't just leave them here."

Margaret interjected, "I love these animals, but they'll eat me out of my home. I think it's only right that they go with a family that has the means to take care of them."

Hailey and Sydney jumped up and down, begging their father to answer yes. Tab started whining and the rest of us started rubbing against his leg. Marvin even managed to climb up on Nick's shoulder so that he could rub against his ear.

"Oh, brother… this is ridiculous," Nick said in a surrendering tone.

"Does that mean we can take them?" Hailey asked.

"Well, two of these cats already have homes, but we can give them a ride. The parrot belongs to Margaret, so he's out. We always did want a good guard dog and he fits the bill for that job. The mouse is another thing all together," Nick answered. Marvin was still on the outside looking in.

To the amusement of everyone watching, the little mouse climbed on top of Nick's head and nested in his hair. Everyone was laughing and even Nick smiled.

"Well, I suppose, if he behaves himself and doesn't get these cats all stirred up, we could give it a go," Nick said. All of the humans clapped and cheered.

"Way to go, Marvin," I yelled up to him.

"It works every time," he called back.

23

New Beginnings

The ride home was a true pleasure. My family made sure we all had lots to eat and the big motorhome provided us with a variety of places to sleep. Tab lived up to the stereotype of being man's best friend, as he rode in the passenger seat next to Nick the entire ride home. Cindy, Rex, and I took advantage of the numerous cool and soft cushions that seemed to be everywhere in the large vehicle. Marvin could always be found on either Hailey or Sydney's shoulders. He had quickly made friends with the girls and they reciprocated in kind.

We followed Margaret and Tango back to their hometown and stopped for a few minutes to say our goodbyes. It was hard to say goodbye to such a nice human and an even nicer bird. Yes, things might have started out a little shaky, but Tango had proven to be a good friend. I would miss him.

Margaret looked us over and smiled, "I don't know what I did to be so blessed by you crazy things."

No, Margaret, we were the ones who were blessed. She stared at us a moment longer and then wiped a tear from her eye. Nina hugged her and Nick gave her a kind pat on the back. She had proven to be a good friend. Tango was lucky to have her.

While the humans mingled, my friends and I had a moment with the young parrot. Rex was the first to speak, "Tango, my friend, you are one of a kind. I'm glad I didn't eat you."

"Squawk! You're not only orange, you're goofy! Squawk!" We all laughed.

Cindy was next, "Well, I had never liked birds before, but you kind of won me over. It was fun going on all of the rides with you. I guess you're a pretty nice parrot."

"Squawk! Parrot? Call me an eagle next time and we'll be friends! Squawk!"

Tab came along next, "The first time I saw you I wanted to use you as a chew toy, but then again I can say the same thing for the rest of this crew. You're a good friend and you're always welcome to insult me."

"Squawk! I may be a wisecracker, but I won't push my luck with a pit bull. No insult today. Squawk!" Tab just laughed and walked away.

I stood there a moment and just looked at my friend. Yes, he was my friend. Tango had proven himself as someone who would keep his word and who stands by a friend through thick and thin. Nothing I could say at that moment would be able to properly convey my appreciation.

"Thank you, Tango. I don't know when or if we'll see each other again, but I want you to know that I appreciate everything you have done for us."

The little parrot cocked his head to the side and processed my words. He nodded and turned to walk inside of his home. The only known alliance of dogs, cats, birds, and mice was coming to an end. I took one long last look at Tango's home before boarding the motorhome for the rest of our journey home.

The rest of our ride was fairly uneventful. Sleep and food seemed to top the agenda: well, that is, except for Tab who liked to stick his head out the open window and let his tongue hang out. Marvin liked exploring the motorhome and liked it even better when Hailey or Sydney dropped a crumb. The only stress we really had was when someone would bring up Mars. Despite reports of harmony between Bella and Mars, I still had a bit of doubt. I just hoped that we wouldn't come home to find Mars had been turned into a rawhide by the rambunctious dog.

It was late in the afternoon when we pulled into the driveway of my home. It was funny thinking of it as my territory. The adventure had changed me in so many ways. I was no longer the material oriented cat of old, but instead, I was a wiser feline who appreciated the people I loved and called friends. I mean, a dog and a mouse were going to come live with me and I was happy because of it.

Aunt Patricia was standing in the front yard waving as we pulled into the driveway. Hailey and Sydney had been tired from the journey but seemed rejuvenated at the site of Patricia. No matter how much fun an amusement park might be, it's always good to be home. The girls each gave me a quick kiss on the head and ran out to hug Patricia.

Cindy was the first of our group to exit the motorhome and she quickly looked back and reported to the rest of us that neither Mars nor Bella were anywhere to be seen. Had my fears come true? Had they driven each other crazy or had something more sinister transpired? My stomach was whirling, and my nerves had taken over.

Suddenly, I heard them. Mars and Bella came bouncing out of the house, smiling and play biting each other. Were my eyes deceiving me? Had I lost my mind?

"Mars, are you OK?" I asked cautiously.

"Why wouldn't I be, Carl? I've been you these last few days and life has been great!" Mars yelled out, then playfully swatted Bella down.

"Yeah, but I kind of thought that playing me and having to deal with a crazy dog like Bella would make you miserable," I said. To be honest, I didn't think Mars would have a problem becoming familiar with my diet, but I just wasn't sure what would happen when Bella was added into the equation.

"Are you kidding me? I had a blast," Mars said, to my surprise.

"Yeah, you goof, Mars is a good cat, unlike you and the rest of your friends," Bella said, jumping in.

"Now, you stay out of this, Bella, or I'm going to go tell my big pit bull friend Tab to come over and bite some sense into you," I threatened.

"Pit bull? Where? Let me at 'em!" Bella said with the classic little dog syndrome in full effect. She raced off to find Tab and to undoubtedly start an animated play fight.

"So, you're not mad at me, Mars?" I asked. I was nervous about his reply. I had coerced my friend to do something he didn't really want to do in order to further my own goals. It was wrong. I was wrong. Friends don't do that to friends.

"Mad? Are you crazy? I had the time of my life. Bella is a nice dog and a lot of fun to be around. I was able to eat a lot and still get in a lot of sleep and play," Mars told me. I was happy. I was happy because he wasn't angry with me and because he actually had a good time.

"I'm sorry, Mars. I'm happy you had a good time and all, but I should have taken your opinion into account.

It won't happen again," I told him and gave him a quick head butt.

"Carl, we're friends. Sometimes we do what the humans do and we plain mess things up. Sometimes we just kind of mess things up, but everything ends up OK. In this case, it all turned out well. Either way, you're my friend and I'll always stand by you," Mars said. He seemed somewhat wiser to me. I was humbled and I needed that. Mars was much more than comic relief, he was my friend.

Mars glanced over, saw Bella play fighting with Tab and looked back at me. He wanted to join in but wasn't sure about doing so with a pit bull, but I gave him a nudge and he leaped off. I have to admit, it was quite the sight to see a pit bull, terrier, and cat in one gigantic wrestling match.

Cindy and Rex approached me and sighed. "What's the matter?" I asked.

"Sometimes it's hard to have to go home again," Cindy said.

"What are you talking about? Yes, the adventure is over, but being home with a new attitude and new outlook is an adventure in itself," I answered.

Cindy shook her head, "Since when did you become the philosopher?"

"Seriously Cindy, what's the matter?" I pushed on.

"Carl, I'm very happy for you that you found your family. I'm happy for you that you've found some inner peace, but I'm a little jealous. I guess I want what you have. I want the big house full of my friends and family. I admit I want it, but I just don't have it. I'm not sure if my humans even looked for me while I was gone," Cindy said as she fought back her distress meows.

"Cindy, don't you get it? You have a family here. You, Rex, Mars, and Tab, all of you are my family now. We've been friends for years and I don't see any reason to change that. Your humans might just need the benefit of the doubt like mine did. Give them a chance. But no matter what, you'd better never forget that you have a family right here," I said.

Cindy looked at Rex who added, "I think he means it."

Cindy gave me a quick head butt and said, "Thank you, Carl. You're a true friend. I think I'm going to take your advice and give them another chance." She then turned and bounced away like a deer in the direction of her home.

"I think you made her day, buddy," Rex said to me.

"Well, her humans would take a step in the right direction if they put some fresh tuna in her bowl," I said with a chuckle.

"So, this is it, buddy, I'm going to go check on my humans now. Maybe they need another chance as well," Rex told me.

"Rex, it'll work out. Give them a chance and it'll all be fine. I really believe that," I said.

"What if it doesn't?" Rex asked.

"If it doesn't, then you have a place here," I replied.

Rex smiled and gave me a nod. He knew that I would even give up half my bowl if it meant helping him out. We weren't brothers by litter, but we were still brothers and I would never turn my back on a brother.

I watched Rex as he faded from my eyesight, then I turned and looked at my territory or what the humans call a yard. Everyone was doing something. Hailey and Sydney were playing in the grass, happy to be home. Tab, Bella, and Mars were running around the yard in a never ending battle for a stick. Yes, Mars was chasing a stick. The human adults were smiling and telling Aunt Patricia how they left on their trip with no animals, but returned with a petting zoo.

I saw Marvin sitting on Nina's shoulder and he smiled at me. I blinked a return hello to him. Who would have thought it? Marvin Mouse was now a member of my family.

I had come a long way in the last few days. I had grown up. I was comfortable in who I had become and who my humans were. Dogs, birds, and even mice were equals and the era of fighting was at an end. A burden had been lifted. I ran over to the girls and I can honestly say that I was truly happy.

THE END

Made in the USA
Middletown, DE
10 February 2019